Home, and Other Big, Fat Lies

Jill Wolfson

Home, and Other Big, Fat Lies

Henry Holt and Company
New York

Henry Holt and Company, LLC
Publishers since 1866
175 Fifth Avene
New York, New York 10010
www.henryholtchildrensbooks.com

Library of Congress Cataloging-in-Publication Data
Wolfson, Jill.
Home, and other big, fat lies / Jill Wolfson.—1st ed.
p.   cm.
Summary: Eleven-year-old Termite, a foster child with an eye for the beauty
of nature and a talent for getting into trouble, takes on the loggers in her
new home town when she tries to save the biggest tree in the forest.
ISBN-13: 978-0-8050-7670-7
ISBN-10: 0-8050-7670-0
[1. Foster home care—Fiction.   2. Nature—Fiction.   3. Ecology—
Fiction.]   I. Title.
PZ7.W8332Hom 2006
[Fic]—dc22   2005035843

First Edition—2006 / Designed by Amy Manzo Toth
Printed in the United States of America on acid-free paper. ∞

1   3   5   7   9   10   8   6   4   2

To Alex, who climbed to the top
of our backyard redwood;

to Gwen, who always asks for a story
when hiking in the forest

Home, and Other Big, Fat Lies

Let's say you're a kid who's small for her age and some other kids who are way overgrown decide it would be the most hilarious thing in the world to shove the new kid in the house into the clothes dryer and slam it closed. I can tell you how to get out of that dryer by kicking and screaming bloody murder so that the foster mom with the bald spot on the top of her head rescues you in front of the entire snickering ha-ha-ha-ha-ha-ha house full of kids.

I can also give you the complete rundown on the most common varieties of foster parents you're likely to run into. Like the look-on-the-bright-side ones who go on and on until your head is ready to explode like a potato in a microwave about how lucky you are that you weren't born a foster kid in 1846. Or the one I nicknamed Miss Satan because she was *so* evil, and I bet she's still alive because everyone knows you can't kill pure evil. Or the one who won't like you screaming bloody murder even when the family dog sticks its nose in your crotch and who says things like, "A little, bitty dog never hurt anyone."

Oh yeah, well, what about the Demon Dog from Hell?

Man-oh-man, I can tell you other things too. Important things you need for survival, not baby stuff.

Like how to jump down from and then shimmy back up to a second-story window.

And how to kick heart disease in the butt. Scary thought, right? But I have the scar right down the center of my chest to prove it.

I can tell you how to slip some *quote-unquote* souvenirs from a foster home into your pocket without anyone noticing a thing missing.

But there are a few things I don't know much about. I admit it. Trees are one. In the World of Whitney, that's just something I never needed to know, so why waste a bunch of words on it? In some places, the people have a hundred different words for something that's important to them. Like, in Alaska, the people have one word for wet snow—say, *oogabloga*—and a totally separate word for the big flaked kind of snow—like *moogablogo*.

For me, one word for tree has always been good enough, and that word is *tree*. There are small trees and big trees, trees that stay green all year and trees where the leaves fall off. Those are called *decidingus* trees because they all *decided* to let their leaves fall off for the winter. And there was the tree that I used for sneaking out of my sixth foster home because they duct-taped my bedroom door shut to keep me from being a *night howl*. That means I like wandering around and making lots of noise after dark.

That's about the whole sum total of it for trees and me.

So you can imagine how thrilled I was to be heading to Foster Home #12, where there was bound to be some real tree nuttiness going on. How did I know this? I saw a map of California, and way at the top there was no big ● (big city) or even a medium-sized • (medium-sized city). Where I was headed, the map was a blob of green with hardly any \\\\\\\ (roads). That meant trees, lots of them.

On a Sunday morning, the social worker from way up north came all the way south to the Land of Concrete to pick me up from my old foster home and take me to the new one. I was in the back seat of her official Department of Children's Services car. My pet pill bug, Ike Eisenhower the Sixth, was curled up in some leaves in a mayonnaise jar on my lap. I was working through a supersize bag of sunflower seeds—*crack*—spitting the shells out the window and sizing up my future.

Here's the way I saw it. There are two true, never-going-to-change facts of life for me. I'm going to die someday. And I am not going to last long in this new foster home. There's no getting around either one of them. *Crack.* Especially the second. *Crack.* No matter how things seem at first . . . *crack.* No matter how much the people tell me they want me around . . . *crack* . . . I'm going to get under their skin like a bad heat rash. Like a rubber band growing tighter and tighter around their throats. *Crack, crack, crack!*

"Can you stop it with those seeds?" the social worker blurted out.

"Nope," I said.

"It's been six hours and three hundred miles with that cracking."

"I need to be doing something with my hands. You don't want to see me without anything to do with my hands."

"Ugly, huh?"

"Very ugly."

By this time, we were out of San Jose, past Oakland, past Sacramento, all the way to where there were no more buildings, where the sky was no longer blue like a normal California sky. It looked like chocolate chip ice cream melted and schmooshed together. I rolled down the window and felt something like a damp rag slap across my face. That was the air. I stuck out my head even farther, all the way to the neck.

"In, please," the social worker said.

"Can't hear you," I lied.

I spotted a huge truck hauling logs that was coming at us from the opposite direction. I waved at the driver, then pulled down on a pretend cord, which everyone knows is the way to get a truck driver to sound the horn, unless the driver happens to be an old sourpuss, which this one was because all I could hear was wind banging on my eardrums. The truck got closer. I could see the driver's face now, and it wasn't smiling. It was screwed up, like I was a ghost.

"Get your head in!" the social worker was screaming. The driver blasted the horn, *really* blasted it. I cheered and waved. My ears were ringing. My eyes were tearing. Gravel was flying. Whoooo!

"Are you out of your mind?" the social worker screeched.

Man-oh-man, what was *her* problem? My nose didn't get knocked off or anything. She pulled to the side of the road, shut off the engine, and refused to drive any farther until I brought my head in and rolled up the window. "And lock the door," she ordered in a shaky voice.

That was the only major excitement for a while. After that, it was just trees to the right, left, ahead, and behind. It was a jungle out there, only not an interesting *jungle* jungle with monkeys and tigers and vines to swing from. This was just a lot of trees. There was a sign that said SCENIC HIGHWAY, and I wondered, What kind of idiot do they think I am? Of course it's scenic when everything looks like a postcard. Only it wasn't my kind of postcard. I like the ones where they paste an antelope and a jackrabbit together so you think there's really such an animal as a jackalope. Which I did for a while. I mean, why wouldn't I?

The social worker didn't take her eyes off the road, except to glance at me every ten seconds through the rearview mirror. "Girl with your kind of energy?" she said. "Good fresh air can work a miracle. This is where you belong, just the kind of home you need."

Who was she kidding? In social worker language, what she really meant was "Whitney, you've already been thrown out of or run away from every foster home in the world of civilization. That's why I have to drive you here to the middle of nowhere."

Home? I thought. One more place where *other* people belong, one more big, fat lie.

two

Finally. We were coming into *somewhere*. There was a green tree-shaped sign that I read aloud: "Welcome to Lumberville County." And another: "Welcome to Forest Glen, population 1,639." Only I read aloud, "1,639 and a half. I'm the half."

Then another sign: ADOPT A HIGHWAY PROGRAM. I don't think I've ever been more excited about a sign in my whole life because I thought it was only kids who could get adopted. I kept saying "Pen. Pen. Pen. Pen. Pen. Pen. Pen!" until the social worker fumbled through her purse and tossed one over the back seat to me. On the palm of my hand, I wrote down the phone number listed on the sign.

On the main street of Forest Glen, we slowed down ("Speed Limit 25," I read aloud). It was a downtown, but a piss-poor pathetic excuse for one. The bank and movie theater were closed. The gas station had a big FOR SALE sign on it. The sign for Carol's Country Curl Salon was still there, but Carol's business was boarded up.

I most especially didn't see any kids wandering around, not one. It was a Sunday, and if they weren't hanging out downtown, where the heck were they? What did they do for fun in this part of the state when there was obviously nothing to do? Did they ever go to the movies? How *could* they go when the movie theater was out of business? Maybe they had mini golf somewhere. I ruled at mini golf. Did the kids here like music? Going to the mall? What mall?

What did they think was funny? Would they think I was funny? Funny *ha-ha,* not funny *uh-oh.* I could usually count on getting lots of laughs, but what if the kids here didn't get my fantastic sense of humor? What if they didn't have a sense of humor at all? None. Zip. Zero. What if they were weird, really weird? Mutants? Weird mutant tree kids who didn't think anything was funny, except making life miserable for someone from the city, especially a new foster kid? What if *that* was the only thing that they *really* liked doing?

And what about the foster parents? What if they were different from all the other foster parents in the world and had different rules and a whole new lineup of tricks to keep me in line? What if I didn't have a clue what I was up against and how to deal with it?

Another thought moved from the back of my skull to the center of my mind, and this one gave me a fluttering feeling in my stomach. Let's say that country foster parents *are* different from the city kind. What if they aren't just a little different, but really, really different? What if they just happen to like superfunny, hyper, loudmouthed kids who are messy and small for their age? What if these foster parents have been down on their knees, praying night and day about having a superfunny, hyper, loudmouthed, messy, small-for-her-age foster kid come live with them? What if *that* kind of kid is their exact dream child?

My legs started vibrating even more than usual and I could hardly sit still. *No! Don't.* I ordered myself. *Don't go there. Don't start thinking like that.* I had to take my mind somewhere else fast, so I started reading more signs aloud: "Edna's Tree Hut, Home of the Best Burger in Forest Glen. Special Today and Every Day—Spotted Fowl Burger. Tastes Like Chicken.

"Burgers, burgers, burgers. I really like burgers, extra onions," I practically shouted. "Maybe this won't be a total disaster after all."

Another blink and we were out of town again. Just when I thought things couldn't get any more tree-y-er, we turned off the main road onto Greenview Lane. I craned my neck and spotted another sign for Forest Glen Public Elementary School. Only, the L was missing in Public, so I definitely read that aloud: "Forest Glen *Pubic* Elementary School." On the other side of the sign, I read, "Home of the Timberjacks." None of those letters was missing.

"Do you always read every sign aloud?" the social worker asked.

"Yep."

"Doesn't that drive people crazy?"

"Yep," I said. "What's a timberjack?"

"Goooooooooooooooooo, Timberjacks!" the social worker cheered. "That's where you'll be going to school."

"No way. I already started middle school. I'm in sixth grade. That's middle."

"Not here. We don't have a middle school anymore. With the downturn in the economy and the lack of enrollment, it had to be shut down. Elementary goes up to eighth grade."

"Eighth! I'll be with kindergarten babies!"

"Until ninth. Then you'll go to Forest Glen High School, which is also home of the Timberjacks. Let's hear you say it."

"Say what?"

"Goooooooooooooooooooo, Timberjacks!"

I threw myself back into the seat. No way. No cheer. A foster home in the middle of nowhere with mutant tree kids was bad enough. "Elementary school! That's beyond the . . . beyond the . . ."

"Beyond the pale."

"What pail? I didn't flunk or anything this time, so why do I have to go back to elementary?" I would refuse to go. That's what. Let's see them pry my fingers off the doorknob and pull me into baby school.

I spit a mouthful of sunflower seed shells out the window.

At the far end of the school playground, the car made another turn and then another. Just when I thought a road couldn't get any more narrow and twisty, this one did. It was the quietest road I'd ever been on in my life, obviously used a lot more by squirrels than by cars.

Tree, tree, tree, tree, tree, tree. I shut my right eye, my left, right-left-right-left as fast as I could, which gave my head a spinning feeling, like something short-circuited. The car kept going down, twisting and down. My ears popped. The social worker kept hitting the brakes, letting go and hitting them again. My stomach was feeling funny.

Something was smelling funny.

"Dang!" she said. "Brakes!"

The car speeded up. I figured I was going to have to

open the door, jump out, and do a death-defying double-triple roll, making it to safety just in time before the car went down a hill and exploded into a fiery *inferno*.

No such luck. We only coasted to a stop in a clearing. It was some kind of driveway. The social worker got out and gave me an irritated look like bad brakes were *my* fault. "Not a word, not a single word," she said and popped the hood.

I got out too and started kicking at the gravel, catching a whiff of the good, fresh miracle-working air that the social worker had gone dingy over. It was strong stuff, all right, the kind of smell that gets on your tongue when you breathe in. It had a tangy taste like honey and spice, sort of nice, except for the sickening burning-brake part.

There was a mailbox with a handwritten sign by it. I read aloud: "This Family Supported by Timber Dollars."

Then I heard: *Whack!* Pause. *Whack!* Pause.

I followed the sound down the driveway and—*bingo!*—there it was. A house. It might as well have had a neon arrow blinking on and off: FOSTER HOME #12! FOSTER HOME #12!

Man-oh-man, I didn't know what to think. I've been in all kinds of city foster homes. Some looked like big boxes and others could have been old age homes. There was even one that was painted bright pumpkin orange.

But I'd never been in one out in the middle of nowhere that looked like it was put together with Lincoln Log toys. Out front there was a broken-down pickup truck with duct tape covering the rusted-out parts.

A woman was standing on the porch squinting at me like she needed glasses really bad. Off by the side there was a boy. He was a lot taller than me and was using an ax on a log. That was the *Whack!* Pause. *Whack!* Pause.

He made one more whack, then turned to look at me like I was a bug under a magnifying glass. That's what they always do when I get to a new foster home. The country was no different from the city in that way. Well, let him look. I put one hand on my hip. He put one hand on his hip. He was wearing shorts and a flannel shirt and a cap on his head. The ax was slung over his shoulder, and I thought to myself, Paul Bumyan. Paul friggin' Bumyan. I knew all about Paul Bumyan from fourth grade, or maybe it was third.

I wondered if the boy was a foster kid too because he had that twiggy foster kid look to him. Someone should tell him that tall kids with the boniest knees in the world should never, ever, wear shorts. He reached down and pulled on the collar of a dog. He was obviously a crazy killer maniac ugly beast. Not the boy. The dog, I mean. I don't like dogs. I *really* don't like dogs, especially when they sniff at your crotch.

The social worker came up behind me. "Welcome to your new home." *Home? Big, fat lie.* She was waving and *hoo-ha*-ing, like I was a movie star and the woman, boy, and dog were supposed to rush me for my autograph. "Hello! Here she is!"

I didn't budge. Through clenched teeth, the social worker made her voice low, so only I could hear, "Go on. Walk toward them."

I did my cripple walk.

"Stop that!" she hissed.

I did my regular walk.

The woman on the porch sucked in her cheeks. She definitely wasn't thinking: *Oh, my goodness. Here's the superfunny, hyper, loudmouthed, messy kid of my dreams.* The dog growled. The boy stared pop-eyed.

"Hey, Paul Bumyan. Take a picture, why don't you?" I shouted at him.

The social worker squeezed my hand. "Don't shame me. Don't shame yourself."

I grabbed back my hand and used it to pick up my right foot. I studied the bottom of my sandal and pretended to spot something wonderful. "Deeeeeelicious," I said. "With six *E*s." I faked scraping off the sole and popping the *treat* into my mouth.

The boy's mouth hung open, and his eyes bulged even more.

I like a good gross-out and started to laugh my donkey laugh. But I guess the twisty car ride did something to me. My belly started heaving. I clutched my middle. My legs went all rubbery. I groaned miserably. Something sour moved up from my stomach to my throat.

As soon as Paul Bumyan saw I wasn't faking anymore, his face changed. My misery was making him bright and happy. He rubbed his stomach and licked his lips. He pretended to stick a finger down his throat.

Man-oh-man, that's when I threw up a supersize bag's worth of sunflower seeds all over my open-toe sandals.

three

"What's the matter with her?" the woman on the porch asked in alarm.

The social worker answered quickly, "A little carsick is all."

"Is she gonna be sick a lot?"

"Healthy as a horse, I'm told."

I wiped my mouth on the back of my sleeve. I was glad that the boy and Crazy Killer Maniac Ugly Beast headed toward the house. The screen door squeaked and closed behind them.

Postpuking, my stomach felt a lot better, so now I could check things out properly. I pegged the woman on the porch as the lady of the house, which is my way of saying the foster mom. I'm real pale, but her skin was bluish, like the super skim milk that nobody in their right mind likes. Her jeans hung on her something awful, which is not something I would normally notice since I'm not a fashion plate myself. One of the top six foster parent complaints about me is that I change clothes only when they get to the point of standing up on their own.

Why? Why? Why? That's what everyone always nags, but nobody understands that when you move around a lot like I do, there's something really nice about having my clothes smell like me. Just sticking my nose down my own shirt makes me feel more settled, like I belong somewhere, at least like I belong in my own body. But try explaining that to people who have lived in only one or two houses for their entire lives. They don't get it at all.

While I'm on the subject of foster parent complaints, here are the top five about me:

1. Big, sassy mouth
2. Too hyper
3. Doesn't always stick to the truth
4. Thinks she knows everything
5. Climbs everything

On point four, why would anyone complain about that, since I *do* know just about everything, except for math and stuff about trees? For instance, I had never been to the country before, and I hadn't even set my big toe inside this new foster home, but I already knew an important thing. This family was poor. Piss-poor. They were poor as rats.

Being poor isn't so great for a family, but it's not the end of the world for a foster kid. Piss-poor means they aren't taking me in out of the goodness of their hearts and won't expect me to act grateful all the time. I hate acting grateful. Also, a poor family has got enough problems of their own so they won't make it a happy family project to turn me into *the best Whitney I can be,* which means trying to make me be just like them. Unless there's a massive amount of blood or the police get involved, poor families usually don't care what I do.

But then again, piss-poor could turn out to be a bad thing. Not only will they get money from the government to keep me, they might expect me to work. Earn my keep. That's number seven in foster parent complaints: *Avoids work like the plaque.* I don't get the complaint because, as anyone who has ever been to a dentist knows, plaque is a real good thing to avoid. Once I was at a dentist and he scraped some of it off my teeth and put it on a cracker. "Young lady, this is what you might as well be doing if you don't start brushing and flossing," he lectured. I took the cracker and ate it, because, as I said before, I like a good gross-out.

But back to the new family. The other thing I could tell right away was that they aren't what you'd call talkers, which was okay by me because I am. Especially when I'm in a new situation. I talk and talk and talk. I fill the air, trying to be superfriendly and making nontalkers more comfortable.

"I don't understand why anyone keeps a smelly, disgusting, hairy dog when they can have any pet in the world. This is my pet, Ike Eisenhower the Sixth. Some people think he's named after a great general and a dead president of the United States, but what do they know? Ike's named after Ike Eisenhower the Fifth, who was named after the original Ike, who was named after my favorite candy, Mike and Ike. There used to be a Mike too, only he curled up into a permanent ball, along with all the other Ikes. Now there's only Ike the Sixth. He's the perfect pet, moves right along with you and doesn't take much cleaning up after." I tapped on the jar. "Do ya, Ike?"

The social worker said, "Whitney is high spirited!" She used the same peppy tone of voice she used on "Goooooooooooooooooooo, Timberjacks!"

There was that silence again. Why was the foster mother just staring at me? What was going on in her mind? I bet she thought she knew all about me. Well, she didn't! Was she changing her mind and wanting me to get in the car and go back to the city? I could do that! I wouldn't care! Did I just break some rule? How was I supposed to know the rules unless she told them to me? Foster parents always have rules, so I asked her about hers.

"Can I decorate my room any way I want to? Can I order pepperoni pizza every Tuesday? Who's that other kid? Do I have to talk to him? Is that ugly dog near death yet? Can I climb that tree? Are there any special refrigerator rules? I had this foster mother once and she kept everything in her refrigerator in alphabetical order, A to H on the first shelf and—"

Rude! Talk about rude! The lady of the house turned her back and walked inside without saying a word. *Slam* went the screen door, and I felt the sound all the way in my bones. The social worker was just standing there, and I was looking at her back, watching the shoulders go up once almost to her ears before falling back down again. I knew that she was trying to decide what to do next. *What now? What now?*

I knew what I wanted her to do. I wanted her to explode, to turn red in the face with outrage, to really haul off and say, *Well! I never! This is horrible! Unacceptable! Whitney can't stay here, not in a million years! She deserves a million times better!*

But a country social worker turned out to be just as

lame-o as a city one. She rubbed her hands together as if they were cold. She cleared her throat and turned toward me with a big tooth-showing smile that was really stupid because I knew that smile was really saying, *Please, oh, please, whatever you do, don't break down in an emotional foster kid conniption.*

Sure enough, the echo of that screen door *was* doing something to me. Hurt and disappointment, worry and sadness, and pissed off, all those feelings mushed together, like a big greasy stew of emotions. But then, the greasy stew was replaced by something else, a squishy feeling in my stomach that moved up toward my eyes. My shoulders started heaving up and down.

"There now, Whitney," she said. "Don't cry."

I couldn't hold it back for one more second. Not tears. It blasted out of me, a full-blown laughing attack, which is my wacky-monkey, cackling-chicken, mad-scientist, sputtering-car-starting, snorting-through-the-nose, mouth-wide-open-cawing-crow laughs all rolled into one.

If you asked me what I was laughing about right then, man-oh-man, I couldn't even tell you. It's just something that happens, especially when people catch me feeling bad. I don't like that. I don't like strangers giving me sad looks like I'm some fragile, pitiful creature instead of the mighty Whitney who kicked heart disease in the butt.

By this time I was laughing so hard the social worker had to pull me onto the porch. "Enough!" she hissed and knocked on the screen door. I pretended to zip my lip.

While we waited for an answer, I ran my hand along the side of the house. Up close, the squiggly lines of bark looked like it was the secret writing of space aliens. That was the first new thing I learned about logs: they're like toenails, no two are exactly alike.

Or is it fingernails that aren't alike? Anyway, I got tired of waiting.

In case you ever need to know, here's what you do when you arrive at a new foster home and the foster mother is rude and you don't know the rules and you're laughing because you don't know what you're feeling and a psycho dog is waiting to attack and there's a kid there who hopes that you drop off the face of the planet: You don't knock. You open the door. And even though you know you don't belong here any more than you've ever belonged anywhere, you walk in like you own the place.

four

Anyone who wants to know what the inside of a Lincoln Log cabin looks like, ask me. No plain white walls in Foster Home #12. Logs ran straight up to the ceiling. No carpet either. I got down on my hands and knees and crawled around for a closer look. The way the rectangles and squares of wood all lined up, it was like something out of a sixth-grade math book that I'll never understand because I stink at math.

I continued my tour of somebody else's kitchen, somebody else's couch, somebody else's dopey knickknacks.

Obviously, this family liked everything spic-and-span, which meant trouble because I'm not. A backpack wasn't just thrown on the floor the way most normal kids would toss it after school. Not even a candy wrapper or crumpled-up paper with a bad grade was sticking out of the pockets. There were lots of old family pictures in neat lines along the walls. All the men in the photos had beards, held axes, and wore big heavy shoes. There was a pair of those same stiff-looking work boots lined up heel to heel and toe to toe by the front door.

I was glad to see that the house had a lot of dark places, nooks and crannies. That's one of the first things I do when I land in a new foster home. I look for places to tuck myself away. That might surprise some people, me wanting to be quiet and private. But just because I'm extrainverted—which means that I really turn a house upside down when I'm feeling wired—doesn't mean that I don't have another side. To people who don't know me, it looks like I've never had a serious thought in my life. But I have plenty going on in my mind that strangers don't need to know about because it's none of their beeswax, which is the way I say "business."

I scoped out my first good dark spot halfway up the stairs to the second floor, right where the staircase made a twist. There was no window or light there, so I knew I would be practically invisible. I could sit in the shadows and think all I wanted.

I could think about how this house might look different and smell different, but it was going to turn out like all the others, the same old foster-home script.

I could think about how I shouldn't even bother to unpack.

I could think about how embarrassing it was to throw up in front of a boy I didn't know. I'll probably have to share a bathroom with him!

Then I could stop thinking about all that and start thinking about swinging from the ceiling.

Whizzing from beam to beam, Whitney the Amazing Trapeze Girl in a gold swami turban, making figure eights through the air, tucking myself into a ball and spinning five, ten, fifteen times in forward flips, with a final triple somersault twist before I reach out and land on the next beam. Ta-da!

That was better. Yes, this would be one of my secret places—for the short time that I would be here.

I butt-bumped down the stairs. The social worker and my new foster mother—her name turned out to be Mrs. Pauline McCrary—were seated around a table going through my paperwork. They'd be tied up for a while because my social service file is the size of a phone book, and there were a million details to go over before the social worker could officially wash her hands of me.

I walked around the living room, listening as the social worker gave the same old story about my health ("Congenital heart problem corrected at age four, which is why she's small for her age") and my education ("A little below grade level because she's moved around so much, but she seems bright enough").

Man-oh-man, there should be a policy against this, a major Department of Children's Services policy about talking about kids and all their personal information when they are standing right there. People should have to pay a gigunda fine, maybe even get hauled off to jail and then listen to prison guards talk about *them* as if they weren't there. I especially hated how Mrs. McCrary perked right up when they got around to how much she'd be paid to have me breathing under her roof.

"Seven hundred eight dollars. Payment on the first of each month," the social worker said.

"That takes care of . . .?"

Food, shelter, clothing, I said in my head.

"Food, shelter, clothing."

Mrs. McCrary was sitting up very straight now, jotting down numbers on a tablet, concentrating very hard, like someone who actually enjoys doing math. "Well, she's thin enough," she said. "Doesn't look like she'll eat us out of house and home. But we're simple dressers here, nothing fancy. She'll have to make do with hand-me-downs."

Like I said before, I'm not a fashion plate. I prefer wearing my clothes a couple sizes too big because maybe my body will take the hint and grow into them. But the way Mrs. McCrary emphasized *hand-me-downs* made me want to throw a whole bunch of dirty old clothes in her face. The next thing the social worker did though surprised me. I guess she heard something in the foster mother's voice that I didn't hear—something sad, maybe, or something choked up—because she reached across the table, took Mrs. McCrary's hand, and said in a comforting way, "Come on now, no reason to act all tough." Then, even softer, "Pauline."

That's when I noticed that Mrs. McCrary had sort of broken down. I didn't know what *she* had to cry about—*I* was the one getting stuck with hand-me-downs—but her shoulders caved in and she dripped from the eyes and nose. She said to the social worker, "Harriet."

The way they said each other's names made me understand that they weren't just social worker and foster mother, how-do-you-do, nice-to-meet-you for the first time. The two of them must have known each other forever. They probably even went to Forest Glen Elementary School together.

I started imagining what that would be like, knowing someone when you were a kid and still knowing them when you were grown up, knowing them and them knowing you for your whole entire life. You would hate the same teachers and like the same kids and go to each other's birthday parties and swap lunches every day and save seats for each other on the bus. You would fight and make up and fight again. You wouldn't have to explain every little thing about yourself. This friend would know your whole history, your life story. She would always know when you were being funny and wouldn't look at you, like "Huh? What planet are you from?"

If you had a friend like that, it wouldn't even matter if you were a foster kid who didn't have a permanent home. Just being with this person, your best friend, would feel like home enough.

I got a flash of something inside me, a flash that shouted *I want a friend like that!* But man-oh-man, that's just the kind of thinking that's best left unthought. Whitney, don't get started. Get over it. Move on.

The social worker—Harriet—kept patting Mrs. McCrary's hand. "Pauline, there's no shame in this. By the way, I caught a peek at Striker when I pulled in. He's such a good-looking boy. Growing up so fast. Taking on so much responsibility. You must be proud of him."

Striker? What kind of name is Striker?

"He's a good boy. Never been afraid of hard work, never."

"And Lyman? How's . . .? He's . . .?"

Lyman? Uh-oh, that was obviously a touchy subject, whoever Lyman was. I noticed that Mrs. McCrary took back her hand and shook off the question. She used her palms to dry her eyes, and then her body went straight again. It was back to business. The business of me.

"There's extra money for doctors and such, right? We're not in any position to—"

"Pauline, her medical expenses are all covered. This is going to work out. Haven't you been talking to the others? The Phillip Murrays?"

"The Murrays too? But he sells land."

"It's not just the loggers and mill workers, Pauline. Real estate's in the toilet too. But it won't last forever. You just need something to tide you over. This has been a godsend. You'll see."

Talk to others? Godsend? And what about this real estate that was in the toilet? What kind of plumbing did they have up here? Mrs. McCrary wasn't exactly jumping up and down with excitement, but when the social worker slid a paper in front of her, she signed it.

I was glad that they were finally done with the dollars-and-cents part because even though I know that I come with a price tag around my neck, I still get a weird feeling when I hear about the actual *ka-ching*. It's a feeling that makes me want to get into one of my dark spots as fast as possible. That's why I ducked into a closet. I knew they still had more to talk about. I left the door open just a crack. I wanted to hear and I didn't want to hear at the same time, the way some kids hold their ears, but not all the way, when they're listening to a really gross story.

"Anything else I should know about . . . about . . ."

The social worker helped her out. "Whitney." There was a long pause. I figured she was looking around for me, and when she didn't see me, she said, "Well, there is her temper. She's a feisty little thing, but her last social worker says that she's come a long way toward controlling it."

Temper, blah-blah-blah, I thought.

"A temper I can deal with. A little anger doesn't frighten me."

"And"—the social worker hesitated—"there have been a few shoplifting episodes. Just kid stuff."

Shoplift, blah-blah-blah.

"And she has a tendency to story-tell."

"What's that mean?" the foster mother asked.

"Tinker with the facts a bit. But she's working on that too."

"Great. A liar and a thief."

Liar? I snorted through my nose. *I don't lie.* I turned deeper into the closet. It smelled like rubber rain gear, trees, dust, and laundry detergent. Not at all like me. *A liar?* I batted at the sleeves of a heavy black coat. *What do they know about me? Nothing!* I punched harder. *I don't lie. I've got a lively imagination. What would life be like if someone didn't liven things up? Boring, that's what! A liar? That just sticks in my claw!*

I must have said that last part out loud because just outside the closet, I heard a voice: "Not claw. Craw."

I peeked through the crack. It was them. Boy and Dog. Up close, it was worse than I thought. One eye was bright blue, and the other was white. The dog's eyes, I mean. At least both of the boy's eyes were the same color, a mix of green and brown.

He repeated, "You mean it sticks in your craw. A craw is the crop of a bird. Maybe someone from the city doesn't know that."

I opened the door a little wider. "No. Claw. I say what I mean. That just sticks in my claw." I held up my right hand in a threatening way. "I feel like scratching someone's eyes out, and if I did, the goopy stuff would stick in my claw. Get it?"

"Hilarious," he said in a flat way that showed he didn't find it even a little funny. Then he leaned back on his heels. "Babe wouldn't let you get near any of us. He's a specially trained attack dog. Aren't you, Babe?"

"That's the dumbest name for a dog I ever heard."

"You're the one who thinks she knows all about Paul Bunyan. And, genius, it's Bunyan, not Bumyan."

"No, it's Bumyan because he *bummed* around the country planting seeds."

The boy rolled his eyes. "Johnny Appleseed planted. Paul Bunyan chopped down trees."

There was, I had to admit, a slight possibility of him being right. *Bunyan* also made sense since old Paul probably got those old-lady bunion things on his feet from walking across the country. I remembered Paul Whatever did have a pet named Babe.

I pointed to the dog. "What's wrong with his eye? Catattack?"

"It's a cataract."

"I know what a cataract is! Did your dog have a *cat attack,* as in *grrrrrrrr.*" I showed him my claws again.

His face dropped, but then he fixed it into a hard stare. "I know all about you. You're a troublemaker. And a liar. I heard my mom talking. I don't know how the city works, but we don't put up with liars around here."

So this was Striker. The famous Striker who was growing up sooooo fast with five *O*s. He wasn't good-looking at all, not with that chin.

"Your chin looks like a butt," I said.

His right hand flew to his face. "It happens to be a cleft and runs in my family. All the McCrary men have cleft chins, and we're all outdoor men."

"Butt chins. That's something to be proud of."

"At least it's something." He paused. He started to say something else, pulled back, but then said it anyway. "So what runs in *your* family?"

I knew where this was leading, exactly where. My heart began pounding in my ears. I felt my stomach harden like it was making a big fist, but I wouldn't let my expression change no matter what he said.

"My ma says I have to be nice to you because it's sad that you have no other place to go."

I chewed on my lower lip. I waited for him to say what I knew he was going to say. Now it was my hand that was tightening into a fist.

"My ma says"—he hesitated, gathering his nerve—"that you have no family. You have no ma."

There. It was out. He said it. I knew he would. I put all my concentration into remembering the words of my last social worker. I let those words return to give me good advice. *People can say hurtful things, Whitney, but that doesn't mean you have to get hurtful back. Take a deep breath.*

I took a deep breath.

Think before you act. I was thinking. I was thinking!

Use your words, Whitney, not your fists.

So did I take my fist and sock him in his fat, stupid mouth like I wanted to?

Well, yes, I did.

But not as hard as I could have. I pulled back the last second and just grazed him. He was stunned. His mouth was a circle. But there wasn't any blood or anything. I bet he didn't even see stars. "What are you going to do now? Run off and tell on me?"

A scowl, a shrug, a stare. "No ma," he repeated.

"Oooooooooooooooooo. Tell me something I don't already know."

At that, Striker slammed the closet door in my face. I congratulated myself: "You showed him, Whitney. You showed him."

Or did I?

five

Back when I was five, I got put on a drug called Ritalin because certain foster parents decided that anyone who is a ball of energy like me needs something to calm her down. After that, there was the little blue pill that I never did get the real name for. My sixth foster mother used to put it on my breakfast plate every morning and said that it was a very special vitamin *just for me*. Like I believed that one.

Well, for a while I did.

So I know all about pills for making sad people happy and people who are way too happy a little less happy. But I don't think there's anything that comes in a bottle that could touch what was wrong with this family. Two minutes around the dinner table with the McCrarys and I was ready to jump out the closest window.

In any normal situation, I was the one who should have been acting awkward. This wasn't my family. I didn't belong here or know the rules. But it was the McCrarys who didn't know what to do with themselves. They didn't joke around. They didn't grab for the dinner rolls. I kept waiting for Striker to start torturing me, but he just sat there, hands folded, like he was next in line for the spelling bee and his word had seven vowels in it. Mrs. McCrary carried in a big vat of spaghetti and put it on the table. She was wearing one of those creepy, pasted-on A-okay smiles.

And the dad seated next to me! He was one of those Manly Man types with a chest shaped like a pumpkin and hair sprouting out of everywhere. He looked really strong in the I-lift-a-lot-of-heavy-things-every-day-in-my-job kind of way. But he was more of an alternate universe Manly Man because the real Manly Man types don't shuffle up to the dinner table in a bathrobe and slippers like this one did. He kept mumbling things that didn't make any sense: "Twenty-five years. Indefinite layoff. Jerk didn't even spell my name right."

"We have a guest, Lyman," Mrs. McCrary said, way too cheerfully. "Isn't she the tiniest thing for eleven? A regular little termite."

Striker gave a snicker, but he was clearly on super-double best behavior and caught himself. He looked down at his plate before I could stick out my tongue. I didn't really care about the nickname because I've had a million of them in my life—Freakazoid, Skinny Butt, Lunchbox, Pigpen. Termite definitely wasn't the worst.

Besides, I was too busy checking out Manly Man's right hand, which was missing a finger, the one near the thumb, only not the whole finger, just the bendable part. Seeing that right at the dinner table would make most people lose their appetite, but since I was born with a hole in my heart, I don't lose my appetite that easily.

There was something else about the dad that made me keep sneaking peeks at him. Usually at foster homes, the dad is the one I get to know the least. It's the other kids and the mom who can make my life miserable or bearable. But this dad was so big—and I don't mean just his muscles—that it was like he was taking up all the air in the room. He seemed scary and scared at the same time. He kept shifting his weight, like he couldn't get comfortable anywhere, like he wanted to climb out of his own skin.

Man-oh-man, I knew that feeling.

Meanwhile, Mrs. McCrary kept fussing, rearranging some forks and spoons. "Lyman, maybe you want to put on some proper dinner clothes? You know, for our guest."

Manly Man didn't answer.

"Lyman?" she asked again.

Suddenly, he shifted his weight to face Striker and asked, "Son, did I build this table we're eating on?"

Striker's head popped up, surprised, then eager. There was a vein running from the top of his forehead down to between his eyebrows. He glanced at his mom before answering. "Of course, Dad."

"What about these chairs? The door over there and the wall that frames that door? Did I build this whole damn house with my own two hands?" Striker was nodding. Manly Man shifted to face his wife. "Pauline, is this still my house?"

"Of course, Lyman."

And then he turned to me and I was looking into eyes of fire, green with specks of orange in them. "I do believe that this is still my house, young lady. And in my house, it's okay for me not to come to the dinner table in proper clothes. Not to shower if I don't want. Not to shave if I don't want. Why is this okay?"

"Because it's your house," Striker and Mrs. McCrary said together.

He was still looking at me, and I know that most kids would be petrified of fire eyes like that, and maybe I was too, a little. But I also felt something else, some kind of click-click-click. A connection. Somehow I knew that I was the only one in the room who knew what Manly Man really wanted and needed to hear. I leaned closer and said exactly what I was thinking. "That's okay. I don't like to shower much either."

He looked startled and some of the fire in his eyes went out. Then, man-oh-man, he winked at me. Only I saw it. At least I think it was a wink. I don't think he got something in his eye.

Mrs. McCrary's look bounced from me to her husband and back to me again. Striker didn't take his eyes off her. She started talking. About sauce. Spaghetti sauce. About the eight-cans-for-two-dollars special that she got at the supermarket last week and how the sauce took four hours to cook down. When she finally ran out of things to add to this fascinating special sauce conversation, she gave a nervous little laugh even though there was nothing funny at all going on.

She turned her focus on me. "Perhaps our guest, Whitney, can say a few words of prayer. Would you be so kind?"

Why did she have to go and ask that? That was the number-one complaint about me in religious foster homes. *Whitney refuses to participate in prayers.* Certain people got it into their heads that there was some deep psychology thing going on. They kept trying to convince me that being a foster kid had made me lose faith in God and just about everything else. But the whole psychology thing is overrated, if you ask me. I drummed my fingers on the table and explained my thinking. "Let's say there is a God, okay? I don't think that God cares much for all the begging and whining that most people do. All the praying that goes on around a dinner table is enough to make anyone lose their appetite."

"Amen," said Manly Man. This time, I know he winked.

The A-okay smile never left Mrs. McCrary's face, but she looked hurt behind it. She laced her fingers and shook her prayer hands in Striker's direction. "Son, can you get her started?"

"Of course, Mother," he said quickly, and they smiled at each other. "Heavenly Father. Come on, Termite, just say it."

I repeated flatly, "Heavenly Father."

"Now just say what you're thankful for."

Mrs. McCrary swept her right arm above the table. "For instance, mention all this bounty."

I decided that it wouldn't kill me to cooperate a little. "Thanks for these buttered rolls. And that jiggly green stuff over there that must be Jell-O. I hate Jell-O, but maybe someone else is thankful for that." I took a breath. "Is that thankful enough?"

"And I hope, heavenly Father . . ." Mrs. McCrary prompted.

"And I hope"—I gave it some thought—"that no one here chokes on this food and croaks. Amen."

That was the sign for everyone to sink into their spaghetti.

Silence, silence, twirl, *slurp*, wipe mouth, twist pasta, *slurp*, twirl, *slurp*.

Slurp!

It was Striker doing all that *slurp*ing, and personally, I have nothing against slurpers because I was a slurper once myself. I was a pro at it, until a foster mother made it her number-one personal mission in life to get me to stop. Nobody else was talking, so I decided to help out the family with a little dinner conversation. I would teach Striker what that foster mother taught me.

"You," I said. "What would the queen say?"

Striker looked up. "Huh?"

"The way you're slurping. What would the queen say?"

"What queen?"

"What queen? Queen . . ." I snapped my fingers, tapped the palm of my hand on my forehead several times, and struggled to come up with the name. "Queen . . . any queen! What would the queen say about your manners?"

Striker put down his fork. "What are you, the manners police? You got sauce on your chin."

"Slurping's worse."

"Drooling's worse."

"Shut up!"

"No, you shut up!"

We were finally getting a good conversation going when Mrs. McCrary pushed back her chair. "Enough!" She put her hands over her ears. "Enough! Enough! Enough!" The last *enough* had about six *E*s.

Normally, I get a jolt of pride when I make a new foster mother throw a conniption. A little beam of satisfaction comes right over me. But this time was different. It was too easy. I couldn't really give myself full credit for making her go as red as the sauce.

Manly Man pushed back his chair and left the room, not a word to anyone.

"Ma?" Striker was out of his seat, standing over his mother, who now slumped in her chair. "Ma?"

Slowly, she opened her eyes. "Striker, I'm surprised at you. Ashamed. I don't have the energy for this."

"Ma, I know," he pleaded. "I'm sorry. Really."

"Clean your plates, both of you. There's to be no wasted food in this house. None."

◆

While Striker dried, I washed and asked questions.

"Are you always so goody-goody with your parents? Do you always do what your mother tells you to do? Good Striker. Well-trained Striker. Do you always tiptoe around your father like that?"

44

Through all my soapy splashing, he didn't say a word. When he found a plate that I didn't rinse to his liking, he held it out like it was an old, rotting dead thing until I rinsed to his high standards.

When we were done, he finally spoke. "Termite, close your eyes."

"What for?" I asked suspiciously.

"Just close them."

"Okay, they're closed."

"Now open them," he demanded. When I did, his face was a few inches from mine. With two fingers, he flicked my temple.

I slapped away his hand. "Ouch! What are you doing?"

"At school tomorrow, you don't know me. You don't see me. You don't say boo to me. Got it?"

"Got it," I promised.

six

"Boo!" I said.

Striker was leaning against his locker. I sneaked up behind him and gave him a finger flick on the left ear. He jumped around.

I hadn't slept much the night before. Too many new smells, too many thoughts. The first night in any new foster home is like that, but the McCrary house was worse than most. How does anyone get used to that much quiet? No cars, no ambulance, no *ch-ch-ch* of a late-night skateboarder. All this nature was unnatural, the kind of quiet that left too much space for my thoughts to roam around free. Pretty soon, they weren't just roaming, but chasing each other in a circle. Here's what my late-night thoughts sounded like: *Weirdfather-dogatthedoor-Strikernotcute-Paulbunyan-newschool-tomatosauce-goTimberjacks.*

I had slept maybe ninety-seven minutes total and gotten maybe another sixty-four minutes of half-sleep. I was sure that the maniac dog was sniffing at the door. Most people who have a night like that stumble around like zombies the next day. But not me. The thing about being a ball of energy is that everything works backward. If you want to turn me comatose, slip me some caffeine or one of those "vitamin" pills that would make most people bounce off the walls. No sleep makes me supercharged.

"Boo!" I said again. "Boo! Boo! Boo!"

Standing next to Striker were two of his friends, both of them shaped like Portapotties. They elbowed each other and looked at me with raised eyebrows. I raised one eyebrow back, then let my eyes flicker all over them. I can tell everything there is to know about someone in the first ten seconds of meeting them. These Portapotties definitely thought they were dangerous and not to be messed with.

"What's with the shrimp-o?" Portapotty #1 asked Striker.

I reminded myself, *Use your words, Whitney.* I saluted them. "It's Termite to you, fat boy. That's what Striker calls me. You can too."

Striker's Adam's apple started bobbing. I turned my attention to some other kids who were passing by on their way to first period. "How ya doing?" I said to a group of girls. One of them stepped away and came closer, but it wasn't me she was interested in.

"Hey, Striker," she said.

"Diane," he said back.

I eased my way between them. "I'm Termite, and I live in Striker's house."

The Diane girl looked from him to me, back to him, then to me again. With her blond hair and honest-to-God real boobs, she was the kind of girl who makes a lot of other girls feel jealous. She was wearing pink lip gloss. She was glossy all over. But when you look washed-out and shrimpy like me, it doesn't make any sense to feel jealous of someone who looks like that. It would take me about six more lifetimes to be that glossy. Besides, she started giggling and flipping her hair, and I can't stand it when girls do that.

I bet she had a big crush on Striker. I bet she wanted to make out with him in the back of the school bus. I couldn't tell how he felt about her. Not that I cared. Why would I care about that?

I waved hard at another passing group. "Hey, you guys! Termite's the name. That's two *T*s and two *E*s."

I turned back to the Portapotties. "Striker and me are like this." I held up two crossed fingers, then uncrossed them and held up the pointer finger. "This is me." And then I held up the middle finger. "This is Striker."

I think that's one of the funniest insults ever, so I really cracked myself up. My foot was stomping, my laugh was the wacky monkey. "What are you staring at?" I said to the Diane girl. She looked at Striker for help, like I was going to lock on to her ankle and drag her down to the deep dark bottom of the school social ladder.

"Gotta go now," I said. "Don't want to be late for my first official day as a genuine sixth-grade Timberjack. I'm supposed to report to the office of the vice principal. Which way?"

Striker pointed left before giving his locker door a hard slam.

I knew to head to the right.

Portapotty #1 made cuckoo curlicues at his temple while #2 gave Striker a friendly guy punch on the shoulder. "Consider the source," he said. "She's one of *them.*"

It didn't dawn on me then to wonder what he meant by *them.*

◆

I was entering Forest Glen Elementary a month into the school year. Most kids would rather jump into a pit of boiling hot lava rather than start a new school in October. That's the way I felt too. I must have started ten new schools in my life, and I don't think you ever really get over wanting to run off somewhere and puke about it.

But nobody would have known that by looking at me. Most people think that I'm fearless. But being fearless doesn't mean not having any fears. It means feeling terrified a lot, but not letting that stop you. To survive being the new kid, I've decided that there are two main social strategies. I'm happy to share them.

Number one: Aim for immediate high noticeability. It doesn't matter what kind. Just get noticed. Be a soldier parachuting into the middle of a battlefield, landing in the muck with a big, fat smack of your shoes. Ta-da! I'm here! That's my style. Don't wait for them to sneak up and ambush you. They're going to call you a weirdo anyway, so be THE weirdo. Be it proudly.

For example, you might try saying stuff that really pisses off teachers and wrecks your grades but makes everyone else laugh their heads off. Popularity is yours. Goody-goody kids will follow you everywhere because they really like feeling dangerous by association. Or, in my last school, I got noticed because I invented eight different dances: the tail-feather-shaking dance, the hula-karate, the happy chicken, the stomp-out-a-fire dance, the walk-like-a-mutant, the dance-only-your-fingers dance, the head-bobbing dance, and the spin-till-you-puke dance.

Like I said, you can get noticed or—strategy number two—you can let yourself be one of those faceless, gutless, voiceless kids and cross your fingers that you're off to your next foster home before anyone even notices you exist.

By the way, I don't recommend the second choice. You will bore yourself to death. Besides, you might think that you're safe. But watch out. They'll find you. And then, you're dead meat.

◇

It turned out that Forest Glen Elementary wasn't expecting me. Surprise! It wasn't the first time I went to a new school where this happened. I took a deep breath, charged into the office of the vice principal, and said, "Here I am! Don't get into a busy over it."

"You mean a *tizzy*," the main secretary corrected.

No, I meant a *busy* because she and the number-two secretary started going through a million papers and file cabinets and then they called in the vice principal, who kept hitting buttons on the computer and insisting, "We must have *some* record of her. We must!"

Everyone finally decided that it wasn't the fault of Forest Glen Elementary. My previous school must have forgotten to send along my records. Everyone in the office was a lot more cheerful after that. Order was restored. That's something I notice about adults. As long as they agree that someone else is to blame, they can move on. One of the secretaries started whistling.

Next I had to convince them that I was a sixth-grader and not a third- or fourth-grader, which is what most people assume when they look only at my termite size and not at how much important stuff I've learned in life.

"Look, I just haven't blossomed yet, okay?" I informed them. They decided to accept me as a temporary-until-my-papers-show-up, official sixth-grade Timberjack. All I had to do was take a card to my homeroom—Room 27—and have the teacher, Mr. Cator, sign it and then bring it back to the office.

Room 27 was halfway across the campus. When I finally found it, I entered without knocking. Sitting near the back was Striker, who took one look at me and slapped his hand to his forehead. I wiggled my fingers in his direction. The homeroom teacher signed the card. I then walked it back, this time getting stopped by two different student hall monitors, who thought they were king and queen of the universe because they were wearing sashes.

Back in the office of the vice principal, I turned in the signed card and got another form, which I then returned to the homeroom teacher.

"What? Only one more form?" he said in a sarcastic tone. As a foster kid, my life is ruled by paperwork, so I appreciated that Mr. Cator obviously had the same voice in his head as I do, the voice that shouts, "Paperwork is destroying human civilization as we know it!"

Mr. Cator sighed and then said with much politeness, "Take a seat, any seat. I believe in honoring student independence and offer open seating."

I looked around. What planet was he on? There was only one seat left, the front-and-center one that no one ever takes by choice. So much for student independence. I slid into it while he continued reading the *Daily Bulletin* fast and loud, like a radio disc jockey: "Important to show respect for our campus by throwing away all trash, *blah-blah-blah.* And speaking of respect, we urge whoever is removing the letter *L* from the word *Public* on our outdoor sign, to please cease such behavior, *blah-blah-blah.*" (I saw the Portapotties look at each other and smirk.) "Next Tuesday is minimum day, so Monday will follow Thursday's schedule, and Thursday will follow *blah-blah-blah.*" (He didn't really say the *blah-blah-blah* part. That's just what my brain filled in when I started losing concentration.) "High school football ticket sales, blah-blah." (At the football part, he actually did say "blah-blah.")

The teacher seemed okay enough. He had a jumpy, vibrating right leg—I do too!—and as he continued reading, I could tell he hated the *Daily Bulletin* as much as I do. When it comes to the "Thought for the Day," I'm usually ready to head for the hills, which is just an expression, but up in this part of California—hey!—I really could head for the hills.

Another thing about Mr. Cator was that he lived for science. I could tell because he had binoculars hanging around his neck. Also, the classroom was about to bust a gut with microscopes and little glass vials and a rat in a cage and an aquarium full of fish. Swinging from the ceiling was a model of the solar system. Taking up most of the back of the room was a huge cardboard box marked EDMUND SCIENTIFIC CORPORATION. When Mr. Cator swatted the *Daily Bulletin* against his desk, I swear the box jumped.

"Finally! Here's something of immediate importance. Today, all sixth- and seventh-graders—that's you, my *Homo sapiens* juveniles, no offense intended, I mean juvenile in the purely scientific sense. Instead of second period, you'll all report to the auditorium for a special assembly. For those of you who were scheduled for my second-period life science pop quiz, I have one word— *reprieve*!"

The kids in the class all went "yesssssssssss" with ten *S*s, as if they had just been spared from cleaning toilets with their tongues.

"But the pop quiz—no longer a pop quiz because now you know about it—will be held tomorrow."

The kids went "awwwwwwww" with eight *W*s.

Mr. Cator held out his palms for silence. "Let's skip this sophomoric 'Thought for the Day,' which is nothing more than mindless clichéd garbage. True knowledge doesn't come prepackaged. We must seek it out, wrap our minds around it, wrestle it down, and grapple with it until we come face-to-face with its very essence."

Yep, Mr. Cator was definitely a science teacher, the kind who has a bottomless pit of enthusiasm for his subject.

He checked the clock. He had some time to kill, so he did what teachers always do when a new kid shows up in class. He asked the new kid—once again, as usual, me—to come to the front of the room and get introduced.

"This is Whitney," Mr. Cator said, looking at the form I had handed him.

Man-oh-man, here it was again, the old, familiar feeling of wanting to disappear into some dark spot. That was a reminder to me to do the opposite and get noticed. "Call me Termite," I said in my loud voice.

A few kids snickered. Let them snicker. I did my head-bobbing dance.

Mr. Cator continued, "Er, Termite, we have a little tradition here. I give each new member of the class a special gift of welcome." He was wearing shorts, the kind that little kids and science teachers always wear, even in the cold, because there are a million pockets on them. He reached into one, pulled out a rock, and handed it to me.

"A rock. Cool," I said. It was brown and flat, and as far as rocks go, not something anyone would go out of their way to pick up.

"Yes, a rock in the common vernacular. But to the eye and mind that is alert and alive, it's more than just a rock. It's an unusual geological specimen that reveals the splendid possibilities of Mother Nature's tricky versatility. Hold it up, please."

I held it up. No one went "ahhhhhhhh."

"An excellent example of petrified wood." He enunciated each word like someone narrating a TV nature special.

"Petrified?" I asked. "Like when you see a scary movie?"

"Petrified in the scientific sense, meaning organic matter that has been converted over time into stone by the infiltration of dissolved mineral matter."

I flipped it over, held it up to the light, and made a real study of it. I wasn't exactly sure what Mr. Cator was talking about, only that this thing that looked like a rock wasn't *just* a rock. That was pretty cool. Like discovering that the most ordinary-looking kid in the class, someone you see every day but hardly notice, can do something nobody else can do, like pop her knuckles and play "Yellow Submarine" by drumming on her belly. Once you know something special about a kid, or a rock, you can never look at them the same.

Mr. Cator seemed pleased with his present to me. "I like walking around and picking up special things to share with others. I have pockets full of interesting geological matter. This one came from the banks of our very own Mad River and is—"

I couldn't help it. I interrupted. "Mad River? MAD River? Like Cuckoo River or Wacko River?" No one laughed. I opened my eyes wide at the class. "Come on, people. That's a riot."

No sign of life. No one even smiled. Even Mr. Cator looked confused. That reminded me that people who have spent their whole life in one place get used to things around there and don't ever see anything funny or unusual about it. They need someone like me to point it out. Mad River! They actually thought that was a perfectly normal name.

"I'll keep this rock from Mad River," I said to Mr. Cator. "Ike Eisenhower might like it a lot." Before he could say the stupid thing about Ike being the name of a great general and dead president, I added, "Ike's my pet pill bug. Named after the candy Mike and Ike."

Mr. Cator rubbed the side of his cheek. "Interesting pet. *Armadillidium vulgare.* And no, I'm not calling your pet vulgar. That's the scientific name." He checked the big clock above the door. There was still plenty of time before class ended. "Perhaps you can tell us something else about yourself. Something that helps us get to know the real you. What makes Termite tick?"

What makes me tick?

"That would have to be my heart," I began. "It had a hole in it once. If any girl wants to see the scar, she can just ask, and I'll show her in the bathroom. It'll make your eyes pop."

At that, Mr. Cator asked a bunch of science-teacher kind of questions, like "What kind of heart surgery was it?" and "What do you remember about the surgery?" and "Did you *really* die on the operating table?" and "What did the wispy white figures at the end of the tunnel of light say to you?" and "Do you remember thinking anything when you came back to life?"

Each time I answered a question, Mr. Cator said "whoa!" Everyone knows that the more whoas, the better the story, so this was a good one. When I got to the end, he said, "I'm sure we have a million questions for Termite."

They were all staring at me like I was wearing pajamas with purple dinosaurs and a Superman cape, instead of perfectly normal jeans and my favorite pink-and-orange striped sweater that smells like me.

Mr. Cator asked again, "Question? Question? Anybody? Somebody?"

One hand went up. It was attached to the Diane girl, whose full name sounded like Diarrhea but turned out to be Diane Reener. She was chewing gum. Mr. Cator pointed. "Question?"

"I'd like to know something from Termite. Does she know that her zipper is down?"

The Portapotties slapped palms. Diane flashed Striker a special look. I considered throwing my very special petrified wood at her head, but I didn't. That's how mature I'm getting.

I zipped.

Mr. Cator clapped for quiet, then gave a deep sigh. "Any *relevant* questions? Anybody? Nobody? Okay, then. Anything else you want the class to know about you, Termite?"

"Yeah," I said. "I'm a foster kid."

I said it quickly because if I stopped to think about saying it, maybe I wouldn't have gotten it out. I have to keep reminding myself, forcing myself: Get noticed! Say it about yourself before they say it about you.

There was a lot of uncomfortable squirming because some people act like *foster* is a dirty word and I'm doing something wrong by saying it out loud—like it's my fault that I had the dumb luck to be born to parents that I never met. Even some foster kids are like that. They go around pretending that they are visiting royalty or some long-lost, out-of-town cousin who just happens to be living with people they never met before.

"Yep, I'm a foster kid." I tossed the rock up and down like it was a baseball. And even though my heart was pounding and I was wishing that just once it was me who didn't have to be the new kid again, I fixed Striker with an especially hard stare. "Anyone got a problem with that?"

seven

"Me too," a girl said.

"You too, what?" I asked.

"I'm a foster kid as well. My situation here in Forest Glen is similar to yours."

She was sitting next to me in the auditorium. All us sixth- and seventh-graders were waiting for the assembly to get started. She—the girl next to me—was big-boned, which is usually a polite way of saying someone's a real porker, only since everyone knows what it means, it's not really polite at all. In this case, she wasn't a porker. She looked strong, like she could lift a truck.

She was also neat. She was very, very neat. I would say she was the neatest person I'd ever seen in my life, even neater than the foster mother who made me rake the living room carpet so all the pile went in the same direction. The way the girl said "as well" and "my situation here in Forest Glen" was a big giveaway. Perfect English and perfect everything else always go together. Her hair was in tight cornrows, and her white shirt was tucked in and buttoned to the neck.

"I bet you ironed those jeans," I said.

She ran her hand along the sharp crease. "How nice of you to notice. I iron all my clothes."

"Even underwear?"

She nodded. "I have my own personal iron that I bring wherever I go. You never know if a foster home will have one."

"So, no kidding, you're a foster too," I said.

"By the way, I like how you said what you said."

"What did I say?"

"You just blurted it out: 'I'm a foster kid.' I couldn't imagine doing that. It's hard enough being an outsider without making a spectacle of yourself. You're fearless."

"Fearless, that's me," I bragged. "Want to know the secret? Take notes."

I leaned closer and told her my strategy. "The secret is: Who gives a flying fart what people think when you're always going to be a fish out of—fish out of what?"

"Water," the girl said.

"Exactly. So why shouldn't I say and do what I want when a few weeks from now, I'll be . . . I'll be . . ." I whistled, turning my hand into a jet plane.

"History. Well, yes, that kind of makes sense. And yet . . ." There was a confused look on her face. She pointed down our row to the seat closest to the aisle. "See him over there? The boy whose hair droops over his face. That's Charlie," she said. "Another foster kid."

Now this was interesting news to me. *Very.* Three fosters in one class. I got the same excited feeling that I get when I wind up in class with a person with my same name. I remember the first time *that* happened. The teacher called "Whitney," and both of us said "present!" I looked at her, and she looked at me, and I was 200 percent certain that we had an automatic connection. Since we had the same name, I figured we would like each other right away and have lots of stuff to talk about. Best friends forever. But it didn't work out that way. After a week in school with me, this other Whitney threatened to change her name.

But maybe it would be different with these foster kids. Maybe this was better than sharing a name. Maybe we would be immediate best friends and they would understand my way of thinking and not look at me like I had just—plop!—landed from outer space. My head was going *ding-ding-ding* with a million questions. I asked the girl next to me, "Three fosters in one class?"

"There's more. Lots more. There's—"

She was cut off by the sound of a big drumroll, not a real drumroll, but a staticky one from a scratched tape being played through the loudspeaker. To the theme from *Rocky,* a woman in jogging shorts ran out onstage. Her hair was the color of egg yolk. She pulled the microphone from the stand and paced the stage, throwing punches with her right arm.

"Timberjacks! Ready to be champions?" she asked.

There was some mumbling from the audience, but not the enthusiastic hoo-ha she was probably used to from the first- and second-graders. "What time is it, Timberjacks?" When she got no reply, she yelled her own answer. "It's Gift-Wrap Fund-raiser Time!"

Now there was a response. Lots of groans, which I was glad to hear, because that meant the sixth- and seventh-graders in this school weren't so weird that they actually liked fund-raisers. Man-oh-man, I hate them because I never sell anything. I don't exactly have a million relatives and neighbors that I can hit up. The groans from the audience got louder, which gave me a chance to sneak in a few more questions to the girl next to me.

By the way, her name was Honeysuckle, not the lady onstage, the girl next to me.

"Who else are fosters?" I asked.

"Lupe, Connie, Josh-in-the-Box."

"Josh-in-the-Box?"

"Yes. Did you notice the big cardboard box in the back of Mr. Cator's class? Josh is in there."

"Why's Josh in there?"

She started to answer, but a teacher homed in on us and wagged his finger. I turned back to the stage where the woman was going on about how some nearby school had sold $7,489 worth of wrapping and pom-pom bows. She kept yelling. Everything she said had four exclamation points after it. "Santa wrapping!!!! Foil leaf guilty gift tags!!!!"

"What are guilty gift tags?" I asked Honeysuckle.

"Gilded, not guilty. Like gold," she whispered.

"Oh," I said. "And why's Josh in a box?"

"Shhhhh," she insisted, her eyes scanning for the Great and Powerful Teachers.

I could see right off that Honeysuckle was one of those super self-conscious foster kids who never got into any trouble. She suffered from what I call IVPS, Imaginary Vice Principal Syndrome. She felt eyes on her all the time, ready to criticize her for *something*. Honeysuckle was going to make the perfect proper old lady one day. Too bad she was only eleven.

The Gift Wrap Lady was now asking for a volunteer from the audience. She pointed to a teacher who acted surprised, but the whole thing was probably set up. While the teacher was getting applause for being such a good sport, I asked Honeysuckle, "How many are there?"

"Foster kids? Like, a fifth of the class. And there are others in different grades too."

"I stink at math. How much is a fifth?"

"There's seven of us. Just in sixth grade."

I whistled and looked around the auditorium. Usually, I was pretty quick at spotting other fosters in a group. First of all, they never have braces, and like me, they don't have the best teeth in the world. I have a big silver one front and center in my mouth. "I've never been in a school with so many foster kids. What's going on?"

Honeysuckle put her finger to her lips and pointed straight ahead. "Shhh. We'll get in trouble."

Onstage, the Gift Wrap Lady was opening a new roll of paper and wrapping it around the feet of the volunteer teacher. Round and round she went, until the paper snapped off the cardboard core and the teacher was a mummy. "That's how much paper is in our rolls! Plus, it is made from 100 percent recycled paper! We are in tune with the environmental movement!"

That set something off! A whole nuclear change reaction. The whole auditorium *changed*. Things started buzzing. The boy in the seat in front of me made a hissing sound. The Portapotties cupped their hands into makeshift megaphones and started a chant: "Whack 'em! Stack 'em! Rack 'em! Pack 'em!"

What was going on? What did the chant mean? And who cared what it meant?

This was fun. I really got into chanting. My fists punched the air; my feet were stomping. I was the loudest in our entire section. Honeysuckle looked so embarrassed, like she wanted the floor to open and swallow us both. When she tried to pull me down, I pushed aside her arm.

The principal rushed onto the stage, trying to simmer things down. He spoke into the microphone, "Respect, show some respect." When the *Rocky* music started back up with a screech, the principal quickly escorted the Gift Wrap Lady off the stage. She looked scared out of her wits.

I asked Honeysuckle, "What's this all about?"

"Later," she assured me. "If you just stop acting like a fool, I'll tell you later."

eight

I didn't stop acting like a fool until everyone else did, and that wasn't until the teachers made us line up single file and leave the auditorium. Honeysuckle told me what was going on anyway. Not right away. I had to wait until lunchtime was almost over for that information.

The rest of the morning went okay for a first day in a new school. I got assigned to history and sat in the empty seat near Honeysuckle.

After that, I took more forms to regular sixth-grade math, but the math teacher went into this whole, long charade, which I told the office secretary about.

"Tirade," the number-one secretary said.

"No, charade, like the game. She slammed down her chalk and waved her hands all over the place until I figured out that she won't sign the form because the class is packed."

With a big promise that I could change soon, they sent me to math (remedial). I acted hurt and insulted, but the joke was on them because Bonehead Math is where I always wind up anyway. Next came lunch. Forest Glen Elementary has a closed campus, which means you can't just wander off, although I don't know where anyone would wander off to. The third tree on the right?

I followed everyone into the cafeteria, which had the same familiar frozen pizza / shepherd's pie / canned peas aroma of school cafeterias everywhere in the universe. Lunch is usually my favorite period, but this day eating was the last thing I wanted to do. The McCrarys may have been piss-poor, but their breakfast table had looked like something set up for ten sumo wrestlers. A big stack of pancakes, a heaping bowl of scrambled eggs, peanut butter, syrup, real butter, bacon, a jug full of milk, and coffee for the adults served from a blue metal pitcher. In most foster homes, you have to fight for your share of food. A girl can get killed by someone's fork if she isn't fast enough.

But that wasn't the case here. At lunch, I was still feeling those pancakes like a lump in my stomach. I stood in the middle of the cafeteria looking around. This is the moment a new kid dreads most, more than not knowing where the bathroom is. She stands there, feeling like she has a big, icy steak in her heart, which means she feels like she's a big hunk of meat for the popular kids to sink their teeth into.

Where do I sit? What if I sit in the wrong place and everyone starts making fun of me? What if no one asks me to sit at their table? What if I'm eating something that everyone at the table thinks is gross?

Did I feel this way? Yes!

Did I show one single sign that I felt this way? No!

Strategy #1. I barged right up to Striker's table, looked at the pile of food in front of him, and said, "Oink! I can't believe you can eat anything."

I would have sat down and made myself right at home if Honeysuckle hadn't grabbed me by the arm and rushed me off to a table by the scrape-and-dump-leftovers garbage station. It was full of fosters—the table, not the garbage can.

"This must be the leopard table," I said.

"Leper table?" Honeysuckle asked. "That's a disease where your skin rots. Nobody wants to catch it."

"Yeah, that too."

"I never thought of it that way," Honeysuckle said in her neat, thoughtful way. "Maybe foster kids are like lepers to some people. They think it's something you can catch."

She introduced me around. Again, I got the excited feeling that maybe we were all destined to be best friends forever. I recognized Charlie, who was chewing peas with his mouth open. There was a girl who had a piercing on her nose that she kept twisting. "This is Lupe," Honeysuckle said.

"Hey, Loopy," I said.

"Lu-pay," Honeysuckle corrected. "It's Spanish."

The girl didn't glance up because she was deep into the lunch special, shepherd's pie, which was mostly a big mound of mashed potatoes. I had a packed lunch—peanut butter and jelly sandwich, one apple, two cookies. But like I said, I didn't care about eating right then. It was a good time to look around and check things out.

At most schools it's a snap to spot the most popular groups by the clothes the kids wear. But that wasn't the story here. Just about everyone was dressed out of a time warp—worn-out jeans that were *really* worn out and not made to look worn out and then sold for sixty dollars; old T-shirts with sayings that nobody says anymore and pictures of old pop singers no one listens to. Nobody—nobody!—had braces. Still, no matter how they dress, popular kids definitely give off a certain aroma, which is my way of saying that they act like their farts don't smell.

"See those guys over there?" I pointed to the Portapotties who were sitting at Striker's table. "Who are they?"

Honeysuckle pushed down my hand. "Don't point! They're Hoppers."

"What's a Hopper?"

"This town is crawling with Hoppers," she explained. "They're all cousins, and they're all built like that."

Lupe, who had finished her shepherd's pie, was eyeing my untouched peanut butter and jelly. I slid it over to her. Silence. More silence. Someone definitely needed to do something to liven things up at this table. "I got a good one," I said. "They have so many trees around here, the cafeteria should serve a corn stew."

Nobody laughed.

"Get it? A corn. Acorn stew?"

Charlie took a break from shoveling peas. "The trees around here don't make acorns. They're not oak. It's mostly redwoods. They make cones, not acorns."

"Wow," I said, impressed. "What are you, some kind of tree genius?"

"Naw," he said. "See that kid over there? He's the tree genius. He told me everything. Well, he didn't tell me personally 'cause he doesn't talk to any of us, but he gave a report in science class."

I looked where he was pointing. "Striker?"

Charlie nodded.

"That's all *anyone* talks about around here—trees," Lupe said between bites. "Logging, logging, logging.

That's all my foster family talks about. How there's no more logging work and how everyone's sure they're going to lose their homes."

"Stop that!" Honeysuckle said suddenly and sharply.

"Stop what?" I asked.

She shook her head. "Not you. I'm talking to Lupe. Stop twirling your nose ring."

"I'm not twirling it!" Lupe insisted.

"You are!" Honeysuckle said, and I backed her up— "Yep, Lupe, you are!"—and Honeysuckle went on, "You don't even realize you're doing it. You twirl it three times clockwise, then two times counterclockwise. It's a pattern. You do it out of stress."

"So what? Who cares if I do?"

Honeysuckle sounded even more like a grown-up. "Don't get so defensive. I'm telling you this for your own good. The area around your nose is all pink. I bet it's getting infected. You have a classic case of obsessive-compulsive disorder." Her voice took on a choppy rhythm, like she was reciting a poem in front of class. "The essential features of obsessive-compulsive disorder are recurrent obsessions or compulsions that are severe enough to be time-consuming. Compulsions, such as the twirling of a nose ring, are repetitive behaviors, the goal of which is to prevent or reduce anxiety or distress."

I turned to Honeysuckle. "How do you know all that?"

"Don't get her started," Charlie put in.

From her backpack she pulled out a book with about a zillion pages. "It's all in here. Everything that's wrong with everyone."

"Let me see that!" I grabbed and started to read the title. "*Diagonal and Status—*"

"*Diagnostic and Statistical Manual of Mental Disorders,*" Honeysuckle said. "Otherwise known in the psychiatric profession as the DSM. I plan to be a psychiatrist when I grow up. It's the Bible of my future career."

"She's gonna be good at it," Charlie said. "She carries that book everywhere. It weighs a ton. She won't even put it in her locker."

"You never know when you might stumble upon an interesting case."

I opened the book and flipped through. Then I closed it. Books with that many pages make my head hurt. "Everything that's wrong with everyone? What's it say in there about me?"

"It doesn't name every individual person in the world," she explained. "It gives various symptoms and then offers a possible diagnosis. Stop bending the pages, Termite! I hate bent pages."

"What about my symptoms?"

She ran her finger along the index and then turned to page eighty-five. "The essential features of attention deficit/hyperactivity disorder manifest—"

I interrupted. "ADHD! Tell me something about myself I don't already know!"

"—manifest as impatience, frequent interruptions, and—"

"I don't need a big, fat book to tell me that. What about the box kid?"

"Oh, Josh. I have him thoroughly diagnosed. Separation anxiety disorder." Then she used a lot of big words to which I said, "Man-oh-man, all that just to say that he's freaking out about being a foster kid, so he tucks himself away in a nice, cozy dark place?"

"On the nose," Charlie answered.

From what I'd heard so far, all this *Diagonal and Status* business seemed totally obvious. But one person did come to mind that I wanted to know more about. "What about this guy I know? I call him Manly Man, but not to his face. Right now, I don't think he can appreciate a good joke."

"Go on," Honeysuckle said, full of interest.

"He doesn't say much," I began.

"Maybe he's a deep thinker."

"What do you mean?"

"Maybe he saves his words for what really matters and doesn't blurt out each and every thing that pops into his mind."

"Naw, it's not like that. He walks around in a bathrobe all day. He doesn't go to work or eat much. And when you sit next to him, he's there but not really there, if you get what I mean."

"I understand exactly," Honeysuckle said. "I know that one by heart. Major depressive episode. Symptoms include loss of interest in nearly all activities, changes in appetite, decreased sex drive—"

"I don't want to think about that one," I said.

"—decreased mental and physical energy, feelings of worthlessness or guilt."

"I thought he just needed super megavitamins for tired blood."

"Your foster father, huh?" Charlie asked. "Mine too."

"You should see mine." Lupe stuck out her arms straight in front of her. "He walks around all night and sleeps all day, like he *vants* to suck your blood."

Honeysuckle said, "It's pretty much all the men in town, and a lot of the women aren't much better. Major depressive episode."

Just then, a big roar of laughter went up from the popular table. Normally, I might have felt kind of jealous of that, like man-oh-man, why do they get to have all the fun and know all the in-jokes without even trying? But after what Honeysuckle said, I saw things in a different light. If all the parents in town were having episodes, what about their kids? Sure, the popular ones were acting like nothing was bothering them, like their lives were filled to the brink with magic moments. But if they all had fathers walking around in bathrobes and mumbling to themselves? If they all had mothers who were acting like rubber bands ready to snap?

Striker. He was laughing too, really yukking it up with the Portapotties, who were arm-wrestling. Diane was sitting so close and was so attentive, it was like she was checking Striker's mouth for cavities.

What a bunch of phonies. Their lives weren't perfect, not by a mile.

I thought about all the signs on the stores on the main street of town. FOR SALE. CLOSED UNTIL FURTHER NOTICE.

I'm no stranger to people giving up. Heck, after what happened to me in my eighth foster home that I don't like talking about, I was about ready to give up myself. But a whole town? Whoever heard of a whole place giving up?

"How did it happen?" I asked. "Is it catching?"

That's when I learned about how I was living in the middle of nowhere in the middle of a major depressive episode.

nine

It was time to feed Josh. Honeysuckle explained, "All the teachers—except for Mr. Cator—say that Josh hides out in the box just to get attention and that we should ignore him and he'll come out when he gets hungry enough."

"That's cold." I started packing the lunch trash. "It's his first time in foster care, right? No wonder he's hiding. What about his foster parents? Do they have the depressive disease?"

Honeysuckle turned thumbs down. "They're the worst of the worst. They talk to him like he's a dog."

"Go! Sit! Be a good boy!" I mimicked.

"Exactly."

"I hate that!"

We gathered up all the leftovers—half of the PB&J,

one Oreo, some peas in a paper cup, an apple, a cheese stick, and half a bag of chips. As soon as we left the cafeteria, I couldn't wait any longer. I needed to know. "So what's going on around here? What happened in the assembly? What's with all the foster kids?"

"Well," Honeysuckle began, "this is a timber town." To which I said, "Duh," to which she said, "If you're going to be all ADHD about it, I'm not going to waste my words," to which I said, "Don't take it personal. It's just me—get used to it. Talk away." So she did.

"This is a timber town," she began again. "Everyone for generations—great-grandfathers, grandfathers, fathers, kids our age—has been connected to timber in some way."

"What do you mean, connected?"

"Some people cut down the trees, and some people chop off the limbs, and some people drag the trees to tractors, and some people drive the trees to the mill. Whack 'em, stack 'em—"

"Rack 'em, pack 'em! I get it now!"

"That's the way it *used* to be," she emphasized. "There was once so much work around here that people had their choice of timber jobs and got paid pretty well for it too. You know the main road into town, how it's always practically deserted? My foster mother told me that there used to be so much activity on it, a whole procession of log trucks, dump trucks, from morning to night."

We were passing the gym right then, and I peeked inside. It looked like a bunch of fourth-graders in there, all in their blue PE uniforms, most of them doing jumping jacks. My eyes went right to the rope hanging from the ceiling. My eyes always go to the rope. Or to ladders or landings or anything else that I can jump on and climb. It was like that rope was calling me. Up, up, and more up, until everyone else would be too chicken to follow and I'd be up there, way at the top, above everyone, seeing the whole school but not having to really be a part of it. And when I was ready to come down, I'd be a flash, fast without sliding, no big, ugly, red rope burns on the insides of my thighs like most kids get. If anyone tried to make me come down before I was ready, I would refuse. Let them try!

"Huh?" Honeysuckle said.

Oops! I had been speaking under my breath, saying what I was thinking again. "Never mind that. Go on with the story. You were telling me about the . . . about the—"

"Then boom!"

"Boom?"

We started walking again.

"Boom!" she repeated. "The whole timber industry fell down like one of those trees out there."

"What happened? Why boom? What do you mean, boom?"

By the time we reached Mr. Cator's room, I learned important things about what was going on in Forest Glen. A lot more made sense now. For instance,

NUMBER ONE: The government stopped a lot of the logging because they found a rare owl living in the trees.

NUMBER TWO: The sign I'd seen at Edna's Tree Hut, SPECIAL TODAY AND EVERY DAY—SPOTTED FOWL BURGER. TASTES LIKE CHICKEN, was what the people around here think is a hilarious joke.

NUMBER THREE: The environmental movement and recycling—especially of lumber products like paper— are dirty words. "Hence the uprising in the assembly," Honeysuckle explained. "Hence," I agreed.

NUMBER FOUR: The timber company that almost everyone once worked for laid off a lot of people.

NUMBER FIVE: Everyone eats a humongous breakfast around here, even though hardly anyone is going to work. It's a logger tradition.

NUMBER SIX: Striker, the name of my personal enemy, wasn't a nickname. It was his actual real name. He was born the day a bunch of loggers, led by his father, went on strike against the company and got better pay. But that was a long time ago.

"Now everyone blames the bad pay and unemployment on the tree lovers," Honeysuckle explained as we entered the science room. Mr. Cator, who was standing in the back setting out bottles of chemicals for his next class, put in his opinion. "It's just too easy to blame the environmentalists. Nobody is willing to look at the big picture. All sorts of things came together to cause the timber industry around here to fail—improved technology, cheaper timber from foreign countries, greedy corporations. People around here don't want to hear that. They need a scapegoat."

"A scape owl," I said, and Mr. Cator went, "He-he-he, I like that."

"So what happened?" I asked.

"For one, lots of people moved," Honeysuckle said. "I've only been here about six months, and I know at least ten kids whose families packed up and moved."

"Correct," Mr. Cator said. "But lots of families are also determined to stay. Loggers are independent types. They won't give up their homes easily. You can't believe the ideas they've come up with to boost the economy of Forest Glen!"

"Like what?" I asked.

Mr. Cator put his hand on his temples and shook his head in disbelief. *Let's make a golf course when no one around here plays golf. Let's try growing wine grapes where grapes can't grow!* You girls might like this one: Someone thought they spotted a UFO around here— which, as a man of science, I must say is complete and utter nonsense. But some folks actually thought they could turn the spot into a tourist attraction and charge big bucks."

I noticed that Honeysuckle was listening hard, *very* hard, to all this. "But they finally did come up with something profitable," she said. "Very profitable."

Mr. Cator started fiddling with his vials and looked uncomfortable.

"What?" I asked.

"Me," Honeysuckle said.

"You?"

"And Lupe. And Charlie. And Josh. All of us." She paused and gave me a meaningful look. "You."

"Me?"

"You. Seven hundred and eight dollars a month."

A *ding-ding-ding* went off in my head. I heard the social worker's words: *A godsend. Something to tide you over.* "*Ka-ching*," I said.

Honeysuckle nodded. "Exactly."

ten

After Honeysuckle told me what was going on, everything made sense. I understood why the McCrarys had
signed up as a foster family and why Manly Man didn't
want to get out of his bathrobe and why Mrs. McCrary
was doing her best to act as if nothing was wrong when
everything was wrong.

Sometimes after I know what's what and why's why,
it makes me feel better, like I have everything under control. But this time I wanted to rush back to the gym and
climb to the top of the rope and stay there. Man-oh-man,
I knew I wasn't supposed to have certain thoughts,
thoughts about being in a family that really wanted
me there. I had ordered myself not to have them, but
those thoughts sneaked in anyway. So now I was feeling
like a complete nitwit for having them. No one had been

praying day and night for a kid like me to come live with them. No one wanted me or any of us to stay forever. Home! What a big, fat lie. It was home just until the turnaround, whatever a *turnaround* is.

No wonder Josh didn't want to come out into the open. I felt like crawling in there with him.

"Hey, you, Josh kid, come on out for your lunch," I said.

"Don't waste your breath," Honeysuckle said. "I've tried my best psychology on him, and he won't come out until the end of the day, not until everyone has left."

"Like a fathom."

"Phantom. *P-h-a-n-t-o-m* is a ghost. Fathom is . . . look it up." She handed me the dictionary.

I read, "Fathom is a unit of length equal to six feet and used—"

"It's how you measure the depth of the ocean."

"Right, fathom," I insisted. "Something deep is going on inside of Josh, and I know what it is."

Honeysuckle placed the bag of food by the closed flaps of the box. We watched a hand reach out and grab it. It was pudgy and caramel-colored. The hand, I mean, not the bag.

I said to Honeysuckle, "Let's hang out here awhile. Mr. Cator's gone off somewhere. It's only us."

"Sure. Why not?"

"Sit down, and I'll reveal your future." I dug into my backpack for paper and a pen.

"Like if I'm going to be a famous psychiatrist?"

"Sure. I have the power to know all," I assured her. "First, tell me your favorite animal."

"What's that got to do with anything?"

"Honeysuckle, doesn't your brain hurt from thinking so hard? Do you always think so much?"

"Do you always think so little?"

"Good one!" I said. "Are you going to answer or not?"

"Okay! Favorite animal. Cat." She watched as I wrote it down.

"Next, tell me the name of a boy."

"I don't like any boy!" She said it too quickly, so I knew she had a massive crush on someone. Josh, maybe?

"It doesn't have to be your thump-thump-thump, kiss-me-honey, let's-get-married boy. Don't make a big production over it!"

"Okay," she said, still suspicious. "Herman. By the way, I don't know any Herman."

"The first number that comes to your mind."

"Three."

"That's the idea. Be a blurter-outer like me. A kind of transportation?"

"Train."

"And the final question: A verb?"

"Any verb?" When I nodded, she said, "Think."

I got all dramatic, swirled around a few times like I was working myself into a trance. "Your future awaits you," I said in a quivery voice. Then I read from the paper. "You, Honeysuckle, will marry a *cat* named *Herman*, have *three* children, and drive a *train* to your job as a *thinker.*"

Most people really crack up at this point, but Honeysuckle, being the extremely serious type, got even more serious. "I like the idea of a job as a thinker." She was going on about how a psychiatrist is really a thinker, when I saw that one of the flaps on the box had opened a little.

I interrupted Honeysuckle. "So, Josh, what about you?"

No answer.

"Come on! Let's hear your future."

The box rattled again, and a thin voice came out. "Banana slug, Joan of Arc, Seven and a half, spaceship, observe."

"Good ones," I said. "You're going to marry a banana slug named Joan of Arc, have seven and a half kids, and take a spaceship to your job as an observer. What's a banana slug?"

"They live in the woods around here," Honeysuckle explained. "It's a yellow slug about so big"—she spread her thumb and first finger about five inches apart and shivered—"and it leaves a slime trail."

"Slime. Cool. Now I have another game," I went on. "I've only been in this school for one day, not even really a whole day, but I can already tell you the top four people in our grade in order of popularity. In position number four, Striker. In position number three, Diane Reener, aka Diarrhea. And tied for position numbers two and one are the Hopper cousins."

"No!" came the voice from the box. "Striker's more popular than Diane. He's even more popular than the Hoppers."

"I don't know about that," I said.

All four flaps of the box flung open, but I still couldn't see the kid inside. "He's popular! Everyone likes him, even if he is different."

"What do you mean, different?" I asked.

"He cares about things, even though he tries to act like he doesn't."

"What kinds of things?"

"Things! Trees, bugs, things that his friends never even notice."

"I'm living in Striker's house, so I should know. He's popular because he's just the same as his idiot friends and—"

"You don't know! You're not gonna be an observer

when you grow up. You don't see what I get to see here all day."

"True," I said. "Come out and trade places with me. I wanna see things from your angle."

No answer, no movement. Honeysuckle mouthed the words "told you so" and looked pretty smug.

"Next game," I announced. "Honeysuckle, tell me about your first foster home. Naw, I'll go first this time. The Amazing Tale of Termite."

I took a big breath to make the opening of my story sound more dramatic. "My first foster home. Yeah, I remember it," I said. "Yeah, I remember being so angry. I kept saying to myself, I don't want to be sleeping in someone else's house, eating at someone else's table, having strangers talk to me like I'm some kind of dog. I hate dogs."

Except for the hating-dogs part, all of this was a big, fat . . . NOT a lie, a lively exaggeration. I was only two months old when I got carted off to my first foster home, and two-month-olds don't remember much of anything. But I said it anyway—not because I'm a liar like some people who don't know anything say, but because I wanted to show Josh that even though I wasn't in a box, I knew exactly how he felt.

I guess it worked because he moved forward to the very edge, which gave me a good view of him. He lowered the PB&J from its eating position. He had on plastic-framed glasses, the real thick kind that make your eyes look huge and startle people when you blink. He was wearing a too-big red T-shirt that said STANFORD on it.

I got down on my hands and knees and moved closer to the box. He inched away to make sure we weren't touching. "Nice place you got here," I said. "I bet you and Ike Eisenhower would get along. He likes to curl up and make himself as small as possible when there's danger. Can't blame him. I like dark spots myself, and high places."

When I pulled my head out of the box and moved away, I asked, "Where'd you get that shirt?"

Josh muttered something.

"Speak up."

"Social worker!"

Honeysuckle explained. "The social worker said that if Josh sets his mind to it, he can get into Stanford. Stanford's a big college. It's hard to get into."

I drummed my fingers on the box. "Must be one of those optometrist social workers."

"Optimistic," Honeysuckle tried to correct.

"No, optometrist. That social worker needs to get her vision checked." I turned back to Josh. "No offense, kid. This thing about getting into Stanford? It looks like you're having trouble getting through sixth grade."

Honeysuckle elbowed me hard. "That's cruel."

"It's not cruel if it's true. That's my motto. He should hear the truth. He's a foster kid, not a retard."

"Termite!" Honeysuckle practically shouted.

"Well, he's not! He needs the truth. The truth will set him free!" I once heard a religious guy on TV say that and liked the way it sounded. I turned back to Josh. "Hey, you, just because your foster parents treat you like a dog doesn't mean you should act like one. Act normal! You want people to think you've got bats in the bell tree?"

"Belfry. Bats in the belfry," Honeysuckle said.

Josh scooted back into the box. "I don't care what people think."

Josh wasn't fooling anyone, most especially not me. The way he said "I don't care" was just the way I usually said it. It proved that he cared every minute of every hour of every day.

◆

"Bats in the belfry," I said.

"A loose screw," said Charlie.

"Psycho," said Honeysuckle.

"What *is* a belfry anyway?" Lupe asked.

We were on the bus riding home from my first day as a sixth-grade Timberjack. Only one day, and I was already pretty noticeable. Sitting next to me and sharing my bag of sunflower seeds, Josh huddled up by the window, making himself as small as possible. Honeysuckle, Charlie, and Lupe were squeezed into the seat behind us, and we were up to our eighth cinnamon—words that mean the same thing only a little spicier—for *crazy*. It was Charlie's turn again. "Fruitcake," he said.

Honeysuckle added potty and batty. I said loopy, and Lupe said "what?" which is pretty hysterical and pretty sad too. What kind of parents name a kid something that sounds like a word for crazy?

"Remember, it's pronounced Lu-pay," Honeysuckle told me.

"Sorry," I said, and Lupe said that it's okay if I forget sometimes and call her Loopy, but no one else can. Then Lu-pay added goofy and wacky, which is when Striker walked by and slugged me on the shoulder. "Our stop," he muttered without slowing down. When we got off, I waved to my new friends and kept yelling—"bananas, screwy"—until the bus pulled away and it was just me and Striker and a few million trees.

"You go that way," he said, pointing right. "To the house."

"Where are you going?"

"None of your business."

I spit out a few sunflower seed shells by his feet. He stood his ground.

"Don't you ever stop eating those?"

"Nope."

"This is how I feel about you living with us." He picked up a sharp stick and pretended to impale his chest on it. He made a gagging sound with his tongue hanging out.

I reached for the stick. "No, no, allow me to help you do that," I said with ultra politeness.

Striker couldn't think of any comeback to top that. He circled me once, came back the other way, then threw the stick at me. I jumped back.

"Watch it. You almost hit me!"

"If I wanted to hit you, I would have. I don't miss. Now go to the house. Don't follow me. Stay out of my business. Can you remember that?"

"Let me write it down to make sure," I said.

Striker started walking toward the big clump of trees in the opposite direction of the house. Twice he snapped his head around to catch me moving, like we were playing Red Light, Green Light. Finally he seemed satisfied that I wasn't trying to sneak up and intrude on his oh-so-top-secret business. He kept walking. Who cared anyway? Why would I want to follow him into a bunch of trees?

Truth is—and this is the ultra-real, honest truth—I actually did start walking toward the house. Even an extra-inverted type like me gets her fill of people, and after the first day in a new school, I was looking forward to checking in with Ike Eisenhower and the two of us cozying up by ourselves in a dark spot. I had plenty to think about.

But guess who was the Welcome Home Committee? Sick Eye Crazy Killer Maniac Ugly Beast was sitting on the porch blocking the front door.

I stood way back. "Hey, you! You with the fur! Yeah, you. Get off the porch now."

He stood and his tail definitely was not wagging with joy to see me. No leash, of course. His teeth were all exposed, like he was posing for a school picture. His *grrrr ruff grrrr* became *GRRRR RUFF GRRRR.*

I took two steps backward. Sick Eye Crazy Killer Maniac Ugly Beast took two steps forward. Then, he jumped off the porch. It's a good thing that I can run as fast as I can climb. I didn't look back. I kept my eye on where Striker had disappeared into the forest, and that's where I headed.

I knew the exact moment when I entered the clump of trees because underneath me, the ground felt like it had turned into a sponge. I kept running.

At some point, I decided to stop and listen. There was no *grrrr ruff grrr,* only the sound of my heavy breathing. I had lost him! I was all sweaty from running and my face felt hot and red, but I quickly cooled down because with all the trees, the sun was blocked. When I lifted my shirt, the cool breeze air-conditioned my back.

As I stood catching my breath, I looked right. There were trees. I looked left. There were trees. And nailed onto a lot of them were signs with big, black, bold letters.

PRIVATE PROPERTY OF
NORTH COAST TIMBER COMPANY
KEEP OUT!
WE WILL PROSECUTE!

On one of the signs—THIS MEANS YOU—someone had added a handwritten word in marker: THIS MEANS YOU **TERMITE.**

Another place that didn't want me around. Another place that belonged to someone else.

That just made me mad. I didn't care about the trees. There couldn't be anything interesting in here, but I didn't like someone telling me where I could or couldn't go. I picked up a rock and threw it at the sign. Then I followed a trail deeper into the woods.

eleven

Usually when I walk, my feet make a *clump-clump*ing sound. That's another foster parent complaint about me—"Doesn't know how to walk across a room without sounding like an earthquake!" But not in here. It was amazing. My feet hardly made a sound, since the forest floor was cushioned with old leaves and shredded bark.

PRIVATE PROPERTY. KEEP OUT. Who cared? What kind of business could Striker possibly have in here? There weren't any stores or movie theaters, no bowling alley or mini golf. I walked. Yep, just old trees and about ten zillion years' worth of stuff rotting away and turning to dirt.

I walked some more. I had to admit it was kind of neat the way the ground felt like the cushiest wall-to-wall carpet ever. I also had to admit that there were other interesting things. Like the way the trees went up and up, like straws sucking up light and sound. I thought about climbing one of the trees to the top. The Mighty Termite in the race of the century against the funny pipsqueak bird that was scurrying up the thick, red bark like it was nothing at all. And who wins? Who? Termite, of course!

"Take that, you pipsqueak bird!"

I could yell in here and no one would tell me to simmer down.

I could say dumb stuff and no one would tell me to zip it.

I could get dirty and no one would care because everything in here was dirty.

I picked up a few cones the size of my knuckle and put them in my pocket along with my sunflower seeds. I spent a long time staring at the biggest spiderweb I'd ever seen in my life. How big was that web? Well, let's say that a witch happened to come along, cast a spell, and turn me into a girl-sized fly. That web could trap me five feet off the ground. "Help me! Help me!" I yelled in a high, squeaky girl-fly voice.

I saw an amazing black bug with a coat of armor, and I thought, *This is my favorite bug ever!* (Except for Ike Eisenhower, of course.) That's what I thought until I saw another new bug. This next one had see-through wings like an angel must have, only I'm not sure I believe in angels. In the next hour, I must have discovered fifteen favorite new bugs.

It was a good thing I was looking down at my feet, because one more step and it would have been a yellow, slippery, slimy mess! By any stretch of the—whatever it is that stretches—this was one weird critter. It didn't look like anything from earth. It was even too strange for Mars. Maybe I would have started screaming my head off if Honeysuckle hadn't prepared me for the world-famous banana slug.

I got down on my knees to study it. I poked it with a stick. The antennae at the top disappeared. Then, the whole head disappeared. "Hey, you, sluggo, which end is which?"

Who would have thought it? This boring clump of trees turned out to be not boring at all. It was packed with stuff. Plus, it was just made for thinking and day-dreaming. It was private and quiet, but not the sitting-still-in-class quiet that makes a ball of energy like me start bouncing off the walls. It was a quiet that made even me feel . . . well . . . quiet.

No one was around to call me a liar or a weirdo. No one was around to tell me I didn't belong. No one was around at all.

Yep, there were things about this forest that I could definitely like.

I'm not a tickler for time, but I could tell it was getting late. Even the most peaceful place in the world was going to be Night of the Living Dead if I got stuck out here in the dark. It was also getting cold, the kind of wet cold when your fingers turn white and your nose goes numb. I said good-bye to the banana slug, turned around, and started jogging back the way I'd come. This time, I wasn't so quiet. Under my feet, twigs were snapping, and my pulse pounded in my ears. No way was I going to be trapped out here after dark.

Then I tripped over a log and really went flying. My hands and knees skidded along the ground before I tumbled sideways to a stop. I was sweating hard and shivering at the same time. I lifted my T-shirt. There were a few scratches, no blood or anything. I sat for a minute to catch my breath, while picking leaves and twigs out of my hair.

That's when I saw it wasn't a log that had tripped me but part of the root of a really big tree, the biggest tree I'd seen so far. I whistled in admiration. It went up and up and was so thick with branches and leaves that sunlight could hardly get through at all. That tree was just begging for me to climb it!

I also noticed something at the bottom of the tree. Wait a minute. What's wrong with this picture? What's that small pile of stones? Why are bird feathers sticking out of it? Why is there a small candle burnt halfway down? I tried talking myself into the idea that it wasn't weird at all, just some leftovers of someone's birthday party in the forest.

But a birthday party wouldn't explain the bones. Nope. Wouldn't explain the bones at all. There was a small pile of them arranged in a neat-freaky kind of way. It's a good thing they were small bones and a teeny-tiny skull, so I knew it was an animal and not a human sacrifice. That made it creeeeepy with only five *E*s, instead of seven or eight.

Hmmmmm, hmmmm, hmmm, I hummed.

Private Property. Keep out! This means you!

When I heard something move in a bush, I jumped up suddenly like a karate killer, yelling aaaaaaahhhhh-hhh-ya! and poked the bush with a stick. Nothing ran out to surrender. My voice was shaky as I yelled, "I know someone's here. Come out and show yourself!"

Nothing.

Okay, take it easy, I told myself. It's just your imagination. Right! *Hmmmm, hmmmmm, hmmmmm.* Isn't that what people are always telling me? *Whitney has a lively imagination.*

But then I put two and two together and came up with four stories.

A wolf who gobbles up girls and doesn't care if they once kicked heart disease in the butt.

A mean witch who locks away kids without real parents in a tall tower that nobody, not even the Mighty Termite, can jump down from.

Old hags covered with warts huddling over a boiling cauldron, and they aren't making chicken noodle soup.

Sleepy, dopey, sneezing men hiding in trees who make abandoned girls go live with them.

Why would all these stories take place in forests if really creepy things didn't happen in forests?

Forests just like this one.

I took off, brushing off twigs as I ran down the trail. With the last bit of light to guide me, I made it safely into the clearing.

twelve

I was late for dinner. They were digging into sloppy joes.

"Hands please," Mrs. McCrary said. I got up and washed them.

"Face," she said. I got back up and washed it.

A good thing we weren't having chicken because I'd had enough bones for one day without more staring back at me from my plate. I slid into my chair while Mrs. McCrary was giving one of her fascinating descriptions of how she had stretched one pound of ground beef to feed all four of us. I tried to concentrate on that, tried to get the spooky forest feel out of my mind, but I couldn't. I shivered and put down my fork.

"Is something the matter, Whitney?" she asked.

"Nothing."

"What is it?" She seemed genuinely concerned.

"It's just that . . ." I turned to Striker. "How'd you get out of the woods without me seeing you?"

A smug look from him and a happy one from Mrs. McCrary. She turned a proud smile on him.

"Striker knows every inch of those woods," she explained. "Ever since he was a little boy, he and his dad would wander there just about every day." She turned to her husband. "You taught him everything, didn't you, Lyman?" Then back to me. "The names of the animals, the difference between the mushrooms you can eat and the ones that can make you sick. There's not much that Striker doesn't know about those woods. Why, the two of them used to spend hours out there discussing the various shapes of leaves."

She handed Striker the plate of sloppy joes for seconds. "Do you remember the time you were watching a bird way up on the top of a redwood—a scrub jay, I think it was—and you were only three or four, but your attention was so fixed on that bird that you stood there with your head tilted so far back that you eventually fell over backward?" She turned to her husband. "Remember that, Lyman? How he didn't cry? How his attention didn't even break?"

That was just the type of story that makes most kids want to curl up in embarrassment, except if you're a foster kid who can't get enough of hearing any story about your personal past. I figured Striker would be diving under the table, but he surprised me. He was looking at his father with his face all hungry, as if he was starving to hear something proud and boastful like "yes, no one knows those woods like my son."

Striker was out of luck, though, because Mr. McCrary kept his same dour look. "The shapes of leaves? The way of birds? If the boy had any sense, he'd be learning his way around a computer, instead of wasting every spare minute out in the forest."

"But the logging will come back. It always does," Mrs. McCrary went on. "You want to be a logger like your dad, don't you, son?"

Striker nodded once firmly, then looked down at his hands, the fingers spread wide on the table. Mrs. McCrary leaned forward like she was going to touch her husband on his hand with the missing finger, but then thought better of it. "See, Lyman, he takes after you. How do you expect—"

She didn't get a chance to finish her sentence because Mr. McCrary turned and looked at me with curiosity. Those fire eyes again. "So, young lady, you and I seem to be in agreement about certain things."

"You mean the bath thing?" I asked. "And the way we both dress for comfort?"

"We sure do." He looked at me. "I hear that you like

making up tall tales. Nothing like a pleasant fantasy in the face of a complete absence of plausibility."

That part lost me, but for some reason, I didn't mind. I liked the way he was talking to me directly, like I was the only one at the table who shared his worldview, like I was another grown-up, an equal. He went on. "At heart, I think you're a realist. We both are. We see the way things are, and that's the way we call them. I think that we both got it all figured out. Nothing stays permanent, especially a home."

"That's the truth, all right. You can say that again." I slouched in my seat like he was slouched.

"I also bet that you like hearing stories," he said.

"True stories? I really like those."

"This one can't get any more truth to it." He rubbed his hands on either side of his unshaven face. "It's the McCrary family history. First there were loggers, and then there were more loggers, and then there were no more loggers. We're the endangered species around here."

◆

That night over the dishes, Striker was mad, the kind of mad when you're so mad there's no room for anything else. I recognized it because I've been every kind of mad that's ever existed. Like in my eighth foster home, the one I don't like talking about much. It was overflowing with dogs, and the foster lady knew the name of each and every one, but she kept calling me Whitey, instead of Whitney. That kind of mad.

I didn't need Honeysuckle's psychology book to tell me what was going on with Striker. He was sick of his father moping around in a bathrobe like a nutcase. He didn't want his mother acting so pathetic, tiptoeing around and trying to say the right thing. And he definitely didn't want some total stranger around to witness the McCrary family major depressive episode. He was practically throwing the wet, slippery dishes at me to dry.

"Slow down!" I ordered, then said, "Guess what I saw today."

"How should I know?"

"A banana slug!"

"Wow, you're a regular nature girl," he said sarcastically. "The woods are full of them."

"I said to it, 'Hey, sluggo, you're so ugly you must be a mistake of nature.'"

"There *are* no mistakes of nature. Nature knows exactly what it's doing."

This was a strange idea to me, so strange that I didn't know what to say at first. How can there be no mistakes? None? That would mean that everything—everything!—has a definite reason for being, and everything is equally important. Butterflies and mosquitoes, roses and poison oak, chocolate bars and Brussels sprouts, cute pill bugs and butt-ugly dogs. What about people? People are part of nature, and I see mistakes there. Plenty of them, big ones. Did nature really mean for some kids not to have a real mother or father?

I thought about this, dried more dishes, and decided that Striker didn't know what he was talking about. I changed the subject. "Do you think banana slugs look at each other and know how weird they are? Or do you think that if you live with something weird long enough, you start looking normal to each other? You know what I mean? Did you ever ask yourself that?"

Striker opened his mouth to say something, but then looked quickly away. I went on. "Today in the woods, I saw this spiderweb. I must have seen like a zillion spiderwebs in my life, right? Especially since I hate cleaning. But I've never really *seen* one before, you know really seen it, all twinkly from the sun. I like how each part of the web connects to another so it's all one big connection. How does the spider do that?"

"What do you mean?"

"Mouth or butt?"

Striker put down a drippy dish. "Are you trying to be stupid?"

"Serious." I crossed my heart. "Does the web come from its mouth or butt?"

"If you really want to know, inside the spider's abdomen are silk glands. After the silk is made in the glands, it leaves the spider's body through spinnerets. Those are small tubes at the spider's bottom."

"Butt! I knew it! What else do you know about the forest?"

"Plenty."

"Like?"

"Like every time you put down one of your clumsy, dirty feet, guess how many living things you step on?"

"Three?" I guessed, and when he said "higher," I said "twenty? Twenty-five?"

"Not even close. One thousand."

I gave a low whistle. "How do you know all this stuff?"

"Most of it from my dad. And a lot from Mr. Cator. He's a really good teacher, even if everyone thinks he's too sympathetic to the environmentalists. Plus, I spend a lot of time watching things in the forest."

"Is that something the kids around here do a lot?"

Striker's look was daring me to make some crack about how interesting it must be to watch spider butts. I could have come up with a hundred funny lines, but I was really interested.

"No, not a lot of kids," he said. "I mean, most of my friends know their way around the woods. They want to be loggers when they grow up—"

"Like you," I interrupted.

"Well, yeah, but . . ." He paused. "It's different for the other kids. They don't really like hanging out and looking at things in the forest the way I do."

"I don't know why not! It's a whole lot more interesting than most places. Man-oh-man, the spiders alone."

"I have a spider collection out back behind the shed." He paused. "I have a black widow and a brown recluse." He paused again. "You can see them sometime if you want. If you're not a jerk about it."

"Are they poisonous? They're poisonous, right? Heck, yes, I want to see them. I better not let Ike Eisenhower get a look. All those spiders in one place! He'll have nightmares for a week!"

I waited for Striker to make a snotty comment like most people do when I talk about Ike, even through no one bats a—whatever people bat—when someone makes a fuss over a dog. But he nodded like he agreed about Ike. It was the first time I ever met a popular kid who didn't think I was nuts to worry about a pill bug's feelings. I decided to ask about the tree.

"It's the biggest tree I ever saw. I mean, really big. Gigunda! But it was also creepy. When you're out there in the forest, do you ever get scared?"

"Scared? Nah. Where you come from is scarier."

"What do you mean?"

"Cars, buses, noise, too many people, the filthy air, the homicidal maniacs."

He waited for me to argue, and when I didn't—when I said, "In the forest, everything does seem just right"— he looked at me differently. Not like *Man-oh-man, you and I are going to be best friends for life.* It was more like *Maybe I won't have to kill you after all.*

◇

That night, my second night in the Land of Trees, it was still hard falling asleep. I could hear someone walking around downstairs. Mr. McCrary probably, pacing, wondering if he was ever going to get a job again, worrying if he and his family were going to have to leave their home.

I got out of bed and tried to tiptoe, but my feet made their heavy clumping sound on the steps. He twisted his head to look over his shoulder at me. He was standing in front of a line of photographs.

"See these men?" He tilted his chin with the cleft at the pictures. "They lived where they belonged."

"Goody-good for them. It's not so bad not really belonging anywhere."

His eyes locked onto mine and pulled out the truth. I said what we both were thinking. "Well, actually, it is."

◇

The next day in homeroom, Mr. Cator caught Diane Reener passing a note about me and she had to write an apology. At lunch, I read it aloud at the leper table.

> *Dear New Girl,*
> *I'm sorry I drew an ugly picture of*
> *you behind your back and said that*
> *your hair looks like a greasy old dish*
> *towel. I'm sorry I wrote:* I bet she thinks
> that pink and orange striped sweater is
> becoming. Becoming what??!! *I'm*
> *sorry I passed the note to lots of people*
> *and that lots and lots of people agreed*
> *with me. I'm sorry the teacher saw it,*
> *even though I still might believe it's*
> *true. Sorry.*

"That's a classic case of passive-aggressive behavior," Honeysuckle explained.

"Meaning what?" Lupe asked.

"It means she was doing something mean while pretending to be nice."

"Yeah, she's probably laughing her socks off," Charlie said.

"Doesn't that bother you?" Honeysuckle asked.

Of course it bothered me, but what good was being

bothered? "I'm not going to be around here for long. It doesn't matter what anyone thinks of me. I don't care. Besides, my hair *does* look like a greasy old dish towel. I never mind an insult as long as it's true. Right, Josh?"

That was the really big news of the day. Josh had come out of his box. "For lunch only," he said. "I figure that if you're aiming for Stanford, you got to start somewhere."

thirteen

A case could be made that Whitney S.—alias Termite—
is a natural-born Nature Girl. Every day after school that
next week, scary tree or not, I waited until Striker disappeared into the woods and then strolled right past the sign
that said NO TRESPASSING THIS MEANS YOU **TERMITE.**

One day, I took the right path and the next day, the
left. No matter which way I went, all roads led to the
gigunda tree. And as if the bones and candles weren't
creepy enough, I couldn't shake the feeling that someone—or something—was always watching me at that spot.

But once I hurried past, there was no other place that
I wanted to be. Mini golf was nothing compared to this!
Every day, I roamed until the last bit of daylight, checking out new and amazing things that I had never seen
before, that I could never see in a city. A stream with tiny

flowers along the edges that you wouldn't even notice unless you stooped down to look. Some of the trees had big wooden bulges on them that looked like animals. There was a walrus! A hippo! There were plants shaped like lacy swords growing out of redwood stumps. A swarm of bugs no bigger than the blackheads on my nose came out of nowhere and clouded around my head. I ran through them laughing, *he-he-he-he,* which wasn't the smartest thing in the world since I swallowed at least a million of them.

Most people in the world don't see the trees because of the forest, which is why I like to say *Hello, people! Wake up and smell the redwoods. Get down on your hands and knees and check out what's going on under your own feet. It's a whole wild world of crawling, hopping, crunching, dying things down there. You won't believe the livestock living under a log.*

One day, not far from the gigunda tree, I found the perfect rock to sit on. I stayed there for a long time, long for *me* to sit still, anyway. The only sound was the *crack-crack-crack* of sunflower seeds. What a smell! I never realized that something could smell sweet and rotty at the same time. It was a really damp spot, so the scent was extra strong and coated the back of my throat.

I couldn't wait until Ike Eisenhower saw this spot. I got all happy thinking about that, how he'd come out of his ball and look around. He'd take one whiff of the air and want to stay forever. I was beginning to see what Striker meant about nature making no mistakes. Everything had its place in here, the spiders, the rotting bark, the slugs. Even a pill bug. Even a pill bug that has never lived in one spot long, even a foster pill bug like Ike.

But another thought followed that one. Poor Ike. He'll like the forest, that's for sure. He'll feel like he belongs here, but I'll have to tell him to get over that feeling— shake it away—because, face it, we'll never stay here forever.

My leg started vibrating. I picked up a clump of dirt and hurled it at a tree. It exploded. Poor Ike. I'll have to tell him, Don't start feeling like you belong, because you don't.

Poor Ike. Maybe I shouldn't bring him out here at all. Maybe it's better if he doesn't even know that a place like this exists. What's the point? Why start feeling at home if you're only going to wind up feeling homesick?

◆

"Young lady, the growths on the trees are called burls. They do get some wild shapes," Mr. McCrary explained when I found him alone in the living room.

"They make the tree look sick. Is it a disease?"

"In a way a burl is related to cancer."

"Uh-oh, can't get sicker than cancer." I told him about my second foster mother, who was going to adopt me, but then she got the disease in her brain and died.

"This is a different kind of growth. It doesn't hurt the tree at all, so you don't have to worry about that. It's more like a mole on a person. Actually, it's one of the ways the redwood survives. The burl is a reservoir of dormant buds. Let's say the tree gets damaged by fire or drought. It falls to the ground, uprooted. The buds in the burl will sprout."

I liked that idea. "So, from something weird and misshapen, a new tree can grow."

"Exactly."

"The redwood is a survivor. It finds a way through anything."

He looked at me, surprised, like he had been caught at something. "Enough about burls," he said. "Don't you have homework?"

"I always have homework. But I hate doing it."

"Go!" he ordered.

As I left the room, I almost bumped into Mrs. McCrary, who must have been eavesdropping. I thought she was going to tell me to stop bugging her husband, but she touched me lightly on the shoulder.

What was *that* about?

◇

"What else caught your eye in the woods?" Mr. Cator wanted to know. We were in the classroom, waiting for first period to start.

I cupped my hands into a bell shape. "I pushed aside some of this twiggy stuff and there were all these flowers shaped like this."

He got all excited in the science-teacher kind of way. His eyes bulged, and he grabbed the chalk and started sketching on the blackboard. "Did the bell look like this? Exactly like this?" He drew and I nodded. "And did the leaf look like this? And was it so high?"

When I said yes, yes, and yes, he clapped his hands like a little kid who just got promised an ice cream cone. "That's *Disporum smithii*."

"Dee Smith?" I said.

"Close enough. Most people stick with the common name, Fairy Bells. And I must tell you, Whitney—"

"Termite," I insisted.

"Termite, they are not at all common this time of year. You got a lucky, lucky break that I hope you will always treasure."

Something wasn't quite right with Mr. Cator's drawing. I walked up to the board and made the leaves a little more pointed at the ends. He squinted at the correction. "Better! Much more accurate. It's a rare individual whose eye is that discerning. I think you have a feel for this. Yes, I believe you do."

He beamed at me like I was the teacher's pet and his buttons were going to pop off his shirt with pride—if he had been wearing a shirt with buttons instead of a T-shirt and his science-teacher shorts with ten million pockets. I didn't know what to do or say. Truth is, teachers don't pop their buttons over me too often. More like never. I usually only hear from them when they're yelling bloody murder for me to *please sit still already!!!* or *stop cracking those sunflower seeds in class right this minute!!!* So having a teacher rocking back and forth on his heels and smiling at me? I didn't know what to do with that. I liked the feeling and didn't like it at the same time because it didn't feel like me. I chewed on a piece of my hair.

Mr. Cator didn't seem to think there was anything unusual about treating the most annoying kid in the class like she was a genius nature girl. He rummaged through the clutter on his desk. "Ah-ha!" he said and handed me a couple of sheets of paper stapled together that were labeled *Common Plants and Animals of the Redwood Forest*. There was a long list of words with matching pictures. Mr. Cator put a check mark next to the picture of Fairy Bells, and I put a check next to the photo of the banana slug.

"You have an excellent start, Termite. See how many you can identify. Think of it as a treasure hunt."

◇

The very next day, I waved the paper in his face. I had five different kinds of bugs checked off and two different kinds of mushrooms and one bird and two wildflowers and the footprints of a raccoon. By the end of the week, I added four spiders, two more bugs, four birds, eight wildflowers, four trees, and three footprints. Mr. Cator said, "First rate!"

"What are these?" I showed him two cones I had found. One was the size of my knuckle, and the bigger one fit perfectly into my palm. "There are millions of them out there."

He held up the tiny one. "In this cone are between fourteen and twenty-four seeds. Isn't it amazing? From something the size of a tomato seed, a two-hundred-foot-tall redwood can grow."

The story about the second cone was even better. Man-oh-man, it was such a good story that I vowed to write it down, even though I hate writing things down because my brain gets ahead of my hand and I'm finished with the story in my head before I even get the start of the story on the paper.

Mr. Cator was so impressed with my treasure hunt that he wanted me to show everything—"make a formal presentation" is the way he put it—to the Forest Glen After-school Nature and Ecology Club.

"Who's in this club?" I asked.

"I am," Josh said from his box.

Mr. Cator turned to the blackboard and erased it clean. "I'm the faculty advisor. Along with your presentation, I have some wonderful ideas for field trips this year. Termite, you're just beginning to get a taste for this remarkable environment we call home and I—"

I repeated with more force. "Who else is in the club?"

Mr. Cator coughed into his fist. "Let's just say that since the economic downturn, most students here have a rather extreme overblown negative reaction to anything that might be construed to be connected with the environmental movement."

I counted on my fingers. "So there's Josh and there's you."

"And now there's you," Josh said.

Mr. Cator sighed. "If we don't get some more members, we can't function as an official school group. Our funding, minuscule as it is, will be cut." He drew his finger across his throat.

Josh blurted out, "Please, Termite, please. You can get anyone to do anything."

"Please what?" I asked.

"We—Josh and I—were kind of hoping that you might convince some of your friends who are new to our community of the unique experience awaiting them as members of the Forest Glen After-school Nature and Ecology Club."

"Are you begging?" I asked.

"Sure am," said Mr. Cator.

"The Termite's powers of perversion must not be disrespected."

"Powers of persuasion," Mr. Cator corrected.

"I must be paid my full worth! I'll take a pass on two days' worth of science homework *and* one tardy to homeroom without being reported *and* one hall pass—"

"What about me? What about me?" Josh pleaded.

I gave him a thumbs-up. "What do you want, Josh?"

He didn't miss a beat. "A sleeping bag for my box and—"

When I saw Mr. Cator fighting a smile, I knew I had won. He extended his hand for a shake. "Bring me the *Homo sapiens* and it's a deal."

◇

We were sitting at the back of the school bus heading home. Josh and I were talking up the Nature and Ecology Club, making it sound like it was a visit to Disneyland and a holiday party for foster kids given by the Junior League rolled into one.

I said, "I'm telling you! Who would have figured? A city foster like me being a natural-born nature person. I bet this sudden affliction with the Great Outdoors doesn't just happen to me."

"Affinity," Honeysuckle corrected. "Your sudden affinity. Affliction means you have troubles or a disease."

"I say what I mean! I have nature fever, and you will too."

"I hate staying late after school," Charlie whined.

"Field trips!" I promised.

"I get sunburned on field trips," complained Lupe.

I countered with, "It's like one big umbrella in the forest. You won't even need sunscreen."

Some of the foster kids from other grades had started hanging out with us, and they were also chiming in with excuses.

"It's too much like school," said a fifth-grader named Connie.

"I hate getting dirty!"

"Gross. Spiders."

"There's poison oak in there. I'm allergic. I swell up like an elephant."

"Are there elephants in there?" Lupe asked.

"Don't be a nitwit," I said. "Just foxes and skunks, and if we're lucky, we'll get to see a mountain lion."

"Oh, great," Honeysuckle said, not meaning it.

Charlie looked around to see who else might be listening besides us fosters. "About this club? I hear that the local kids kidnap and torture anyone who joins. They turn into animals at the mention of the word *ecol-*

ogy. That's why there aren't any members. No one dares join."

Lupe added, "I heard that three foster kids disappeared like that." She snapped her fingers, then started twirling her nose ring, which meant she was really jittery.

"The popular theory is that the Hoppers got to them one day after school. Their social workers never saw them again," Honeysuckle said.

"Come on. You believe that? They must have run away," I insisted. "Foster kids are always running away. Nothing's more fun than blowing out of a foster home."

Nobody started bragging about the time *they* ran away. We passed the next few stops in silence, which was a bad sign. That meant they were all thinking too much. I was really going to have to work to sign them up. When it was time for me to get off the bus, I left them with some parting words: "Secret club handshakes. Double-secret club passwords!"

When the bus pulled away, Honeysuckle was standing next to me. I'd gotten so caught up in my job of membership coagulator that I almost forgot she had gotten permission from her foster family to come home with me after school.

"So that's it?" she asked, pointing to Foster Home #12. As usual, the dog was on the porch. "And that's—"

"Yep. Sick Eye Crazy Killer Maniac Ugly Beast."

"He doesn't look so bad to me. In fact, he looks kind of cute."

"Cute?" I exploded. "You haven't seen that dog's drool up close."

"I don't get it. You're scared of an old dog. Yet you're not bothered by the possibility of mountain lions?"

"I don't give a spider's butt about any old mountain lion."

She pointed to the woods. "Come on, admit it. Don't you ever get scared out there alone?"

"Where we come from is scarier," I said. "Cars, buses, noise, too many people, the filthy air, the homicidal maniacs."

"Termite, what are you talking about?"

"I'm not sure," I admitted. "It sounded pretty good when Striker said it."

"So what's this big secret you want to show me?"

"Wait until you see it! I can't stop thinking about it, not since I first laid my eyes on it. Well, I didn't really take out my eyes and lay them—"

"It's just an expression, Termite. I get what you mean." She paused and glanced nervously at the McCrary front porch. "You sure we won't get in trouble?"

"Don't you ever stop worrying about getting in trouble?"

"Not really," she said. "We won't get lost, will we?"

"Naw, I know these woods like the—what do I know them like?"

"Like the back of your hand. And I really hope you do."

I took Honeysuckle by the hand and set off to give her a personal tour of Forest Glen's most mysterious mystery spot.

fourteen

"You're gonna thank me for this," I said.

"For what? Getting my good shoes covered with mud and my hair full of cobwebs? For the memorable experience of breathing in bugs?"

"You sneezed them right out!"

About an hour earlier, Honeysuckle and I had entered the woods. The forest was the perfect place for having a conversation, not just any blah-blah but the deep kind that you don't have with just anyone. We talked about the really terrible foster homes we had lived in, friends we missed, families that didn't want to adopt us, social workers who disappointed us, whether sunflower seeds are best with or without jalapeño flavoring. (With!)

For two people as different as apple pie and cabbage, there were so many things we agreed on. Plus, we had no trouble keeping the talk going. That's because Honeysuckle and I clicked. How and why people click is one of those mysteries of life, but when you do, you can blab forever. One topic connected to another like the spiderwebs we kept bumping into. If you've ever clicked with someone, you know exactly what I mean and how amazing it is. You never want it to stop.

"I'm ready with this week's Top Ten most popular sixth-graders at Forest Glen Elementary," I announced. "Diarrhea moves down three notches. Striker climbs to number one. And, Honeysuckle, you're number eight."

She stuck out her lower lip. "How can you just decide something like that? Do you pull it out of thin air? You're a new kid here. And a foster. No one cares what you think."

We walked a little more. I spit out some shells. Honeysuckle was muttering to herself. Another minute passed. "Really?" she finally said. "Number eight?"

"Yeah. And this week, I cracked the number-ten spot. There's only one way for us to go."

"Up?" she asked hopefully. I gave a thumbs-up.

After walking and talking for another half hour or so, it hit me that maybe I wasn't 200 percent certain exactly where we were. Certain doubts began creeping into my mind. I was thinking that we should have gotten to the gigunda tree by now. I always got to the tree. I couldn't avoid it. Hmmm. Maybe we shouldn't have crossed that first stream because maybe it was the second stream I'd crossed before. And maybe the shortcut I took wasn't a shortcut at all.

It's a true fact of the forest that once you look at a redwood tree, really look at it, each tree has its own features the same as people do. But when you get into a panicky fear-of-being-lost-in-the-woods-forever frame of mind, every tree looks alike. To be honest, the past five minutes of walking felt like about five hours because I was trying hard to pretend that I was totally in charge of the situation.

"Are we there yet?" Honeysuckle joked, imitating a kid on a long car ride.

"Ha," I said. "Hahahahahaha."

We got to a spot on the trail that was blocked by a branch of a redwood growing over it. While Honeysuckle limboed under, my head was going *ding-ding-ding*-trouble-trouble-panic-panic because I didn't remember any previous limboing. She caught the confusion on my face. "Is everything all right?"

"Everything is *great*! We're having *fun*! Aren't we having fun? This is a *blast*! No one else we know is having this much fun."

"Tell me the truth. Are we lost?"

"Lost? Any minute now, you're going to say to me, Oh-TermitehowcouldIhavedoubtedyouwhatanexperience-

thankyouthankyouthankyouTermiteforgrantingmethe-
privilegeofaccompanyingyouonthisjourney."

"We're lost," she said.

She plopped down on a log without even checking it for bugs. Her upper lip had a thin mustache of dirt. Her light-colored shoes were now brown. "You're in denial," she said. "A classic case of ignoring the facts, even when they're right in your face." She brushed off a bug that was climbing into her nose.

I tried to get her mind on a different subject by pointing out a little brown bird that was scurrying up a tree and making a noise that sounded like the word *see,* but with six *E*s. *Seeeeee!* She didn't look. Then, with lots of excitement, I pointed out something brown on the ground with a slimy texture. "I don't know what that is, but I know it's something."

"We should have brought a cell phone, but I don't have a cell phone." She checked her watch.

"Don't worry. We'll be back before we're ballooned in darkness."

"Cocooned in darkness," she corrected.

"Yeah, cocooned! I bet butterflies live in here too. Nature places always have butterflies and—"

"I don't care about butterflies! I just want to get out of here. I am going to get in sooooo much trouble with my foster parents."

It was sooooo pathetic with five *O*s how Honeysuckle

was more scared of her foster parents than being a midnight snack for a mountain lion. I started kicking at the soil.

That's when I saw it. Half buried was a pile of sunflower seed shells, then another handful and another and then a whole trail of little piles. Man-oh-man, this meant that we weren't officially lost at all. Without even planning ahead, I'd pulled off something smarter than Hansel and Gretel, who used bread crumbs. What bird would be interested in picking off empty shells?

I pulled at Honeysuckle's arm. "Up and—up and what?"

"Away?" she asked hopefully.

"Naw. Up and—"

"Up and at 'em?"

"Yeah, up and atom. 'Cause what I'm going to show you will blow you away!"

I took off quickly, my feet following the trail of shells. Honeysuckle scrambled to keep up. We rounded a bend, and there it was, the gigunda tree, rising up like it was having a good conversation with the sky. She shaded her eyes and tilted back her head to look at the very top.

"Look!" I insisted.

"I'm looking. That's a huge tree, all right. Really huge! Like the Big Daddy of the whole forest."

"Perfect," I said. "The Big Daddy! But that's not all I mean. Look lower."

She tilted her head down.

"Lower, no, more lower!"

"I'm looking and I don't . . ." Her sentence trailed off. She stared at the bottom of the tree for a while, then turned to me, looked back, and blinked a couple of times. "What"—she took a deep inhale—"is"—then she exhaled—"that stuff?"

"Bones," I said.

She grabbed my hand. "Human?"

"Too small, I think."

"What about toes? Toe bones are small." She shuddered.

"What do you make of this stuff?" I pulled her a little closer to the tree. "Why would someone stick feathers there? Is it some kind of signal?" We inched closer. "And a candle. Quick, make a note!"

"I don't have anything to write with!"

"Make a note in your brain. Clue number one: same bones as I saw before and the same feathers. Only now there's a different candle."

"Noted," she said. "What do you think it is? Voodoo?"

"Maybe that. Maybe a psycho killer. Or maybe it's some kind of vitual."

"Ritual?" When I shook my head no, she tried "vigil?"

That's it. "A vigil. Definitely." I paused. "What is a vigil, anyway?"

"When someone keeps watch over something."

"Yeah, a vigil."

"So what's being watched over?"

We crept closer. She said, "Psychology has a *lot* to say about a person who would make something like *this*." She reached down.

"Don't touch anything," I hissed.

"Why not?"

"Because someone else is here."

Her hand froze in place. Then her whole body jumped back. She grabbed my arm. "Who?" she whispered. "Where?"

"Everywhere. It's everywhere." I put my finger to my lips and then to my ear. I pointed to my back, which meant that I wanted her to cover it. She nodded. I began tiptoeing around the tree. By the time I got back to her, I realized that I didn't have that creepy, looked-at, spied-on feeling. It was the first time I'd been near the tree without feeling it.

A big bird—but not as big as a turkey, more like a parrot—with black and blue feathers landed by the vigil and made a loud *shock-shock-shock* sound, which reminded me of foster father number six when he was scolding me. The bird was already checked off on my list, and his name was Steller's jay.

"Ah-ha," I said.

"Ah-ha what?" There was panic on Honeysuckle's face.

"Ah-ha, relax. The other thing isn't here."

"What other thing?"

"The thing that hides and spies."

"Is it human or otherwise?"

"I don't know," I admitted. "But it's not here now, so this is our chance. Take something."

"Why?"

"For scientific purposes."

"Are you nuts?"

I shooed away the jay and picked up one of the bones. It felt so alive, I swear my fingers tingled. Next I picked up a feather and slipped both of them into my pocket.

fifteen

By the time we got out of the woods and Honeysuckle went home, I was late for dinner again, this time really late. No one was around. I looked in the refrigerator and found a burrito wrapped in tinfoil with my name on it. That was a decent thing for Mrs. McCrary to do, and it made me feel better about her, especially since most foster parents have a rule about missing meals. They like to say, "What do you think, I'm running a restaurant around here?"

I unwrapped the burrito and popped it into the microwave, heated it up, and wolfed it down. I had more important things on my mind than food, which is different than most sixth-graders, who think about food from morning until night. In my mind, a whole bunch of questions whirled around.

What is going on at that tree? What if the turnaround

comes and I get sent away and never find out? Candles? Vigil? How do I convince Honeysuckle and the rest of the fosters to join the Forest Glen After-school Nature and Ecology Club?

I picked up Ike Eisenhower, and we went to my thinking place in the middle of the staircase. I started telling him about the little bird I'd watched creeping up a tree saying *seeeeee!* The bird's official name was brown creeper. I put a checkmark next to its picture. What would it be like, spending your entire life in the Big Daddy tree?

Termite the amazing human creeper inching her way up, then leaping from branch to branch until she's at the very top and nothing is above her and she can see for miles and miles. No one has the guts to try and get her down. No one even knows that she's up there. It's her world, hers alone.

Would I be able to breathe up there? What's the weather like? What would happen if I spit down and it landed on someone's head? *Hmmm. I wonder if Forest Glen Elementary has a science fair because if they do, that would be the perfect experiment: How High Can a Spitball Drop Before It Knocks Someone into a Coma?*

Ahhhhh! Someone had sneaked up on me. Talk about a spitball! Drool! I whipped around and came face-to-face with the thick tongue and weird white eye of Sick Eye Crazy Killer Maniac Ugly Beast.

"Go away, you, you SICKMUB!" I hissed. The dog

didn't budge. *"Sssssss!"* All that did was make him get closer and hedge me into the corner. I tried "beat it!" I added the dog's real name: "Babe, beat it, Babe!" But that backfired. He slobbered on my hand—a taste test—then plopped his head on my lap. It was as heavy as a bowling ball. I didn't move, not a muscle. Every once in a while, the dog raised his head and used his good eye to check out me and Ike Eisenhower. Ike's no dummy. He curled into a ball and hid behind the Mad River rock. I had no place to hide. I had to sit there, hemmed in by dog breath, as petrified as that chunk of wood.

This was when the front door opened, then slammed closed. Voices floated up from the living room. It was Mr. and Mrs. McCrary. They were talking softly, and when you hear foster parents whisper like that, that's the time to shut up and really listen. Lots of the time, they're talking about you, how you don't fit in, how you're driving them crazy, how they're going to call the social worker. That's important information to have. I warned the dog, "Sickmub, no funny business." Then I listened hard, like I was squinting my ears.

Mrs. McCrary said, "I know just the thought kills you, Lyman."

The thought of what?

Mr. McCrary said, "It's necessary."

What's necessary?

She said, "Poor Striker. You know how he feels about it."

Feels about what?

He said, "It's necessary."

Stop repeating yourself!

She said, "Isn't there some other—"

He said, "Another way? Pauline, I'm a realist. I have to be."

The realist thing again.

She said, "I know, Lyman. I know."

Know what? What does she know? Spit it out already!

He said, "What? I'm a devil with a chainsaw because I need to feed—"

The front door opened again. "I'm home," Striker yelled. That put the brakes on the adult talk. "Hi, Mom, Dad."

At the sound of Striker's voice, the weight of Sickmub's head lifted from my lap. Thank goodness!

"Where's Babe?" Striker asked.

The dog stood, looked at me, hesitated, glanced down the stairs, then back at me again. *Just scram,* I prayed.

"Come on, boy! I'm home," Striker called.

Finally. The dog inched away. I was safe. But just before that beast bounded down the stairs, tail wagging, he gave me one more look. Man-oh-man, I didn't know what to make of it. It wasn't an I-can't-wait-to-take-a-

chunk-out-of-your-leg look. I swear that dog was looking at me like he wasn't sure he wanted to leave my lap.
Like we were best friends. Like *I* was Paul friggin' Bunyan.

Something inside of me went soft. Maybe I kind of
liked that look.

Maybe I even missed the warm spot on my lap.

Maybe. Just a little. But for only a second.

◇

Along with "What do you think, I'm running a restaurant around here?" here are other things that foster parents like to say:

"You'll be sorry!"

"You won't get away with this!"

"Watch it! You're going to get hurt!"

"Don't tell anyone about this!"

"You're driving me crazy!"

"Do as I do, not as I say." Wait. I think it's the other
way around.

"You are so lucky to be here and not somewhere else."

◇

That night, Honeysuckle phoned. I told her all about the
conversation I had just overheard and how it was making me crazy not to know what was going on.

"There's been whispering here too," she said. "But
it's not nice to eavesdrop."

"You better eavesdrop! We need to know what's going on. It could be the turnaround! The foster kid is always the last to know. We can't be caught with our pants . . . with our pants what?"

"With our pants down."

"Definitely not that!"

"Okay, I'll snoop around."

"Promise?"

"Yes!"

There were background voices from Honeysuckle's end, and when I asked, "Who's that? Who just came in?" she said, "I have to talk fast. They don't like me tying up the phone. But I need to say something about that tree. Termite, I can't stop thinking about it. I'll never go back there. Never!"

"I'm not scared of any old voodooist!"

"Termite, you're not scared of anything. But I am. By the way, I don't think there's such a word as *voodooist.*"

"Why wouldn't there be that word?"

"I don't know. Look it up in the dictionary. Gotta go now."

We both hung up.

◇

If you don't like looking things up in the dictionary, I'm on your side. It usually takes forever, and by the time I get around to it, I forget what I was looking up anyway.

This time, though, I dug right into my backpack and found the dictionary at the bottom, along with some pens I thought I had lost and a two-day-old peanut butter sandwich.

I knew it! There is a word *voodooist!* It was right there on page 1,322 with *voodoo, voodoos, voodooed, voodooing, voodooism,* and *voodooistic.*

Voodooist: "One who practices voodoo." See what I mean? That is exactly what I hate about dictionaries because then I had to go back and find out what *voodoo* means: "A belief characterized by the power of charms, fetishes, spells or curses to hold magic powers."

I was about to look up the word *fetish,* but I got distracted. Right above *voodoo,* I found *vomitus. Vomitory. Vomitorium. Vomiter. Vomit.*

That sent my interest in a whole other direction, and I forgot all about math homework, which meant that the next day I got after-school detention. It was worth it. Page 1,322 has got to be the best page of the dictionary ever. I recommend it.

Sixteen

I vowed to write down this story before I forgot, so here goes.

The Story of Tree Cone #2

By Termite, in her own words with help from Mr. Cator

The story takes place a long time ago, before Striker's ancestors started logging, even before the Native Americans who say that they're the originals but what about the mountain lions, birds, and bugs?

When the story starts, there is snow and ice—hail ice—not the big mountains of ice that moved along real slow and killed everything dead as a doorknob. This story takes place before doorknobs, of course. There aren't even any doors. There are trees and lizards, bears, squirrels, rabbits, and coyotes. Probably there are earwigs too because earwigs are everywhere always. It's not part of this story, but adults are wrong when they say that an earwig will crawl into your ear and build a nest in the wax if you don't clean them. Not true. I tried it when I was about six. An earwig will crawl right out, even if you try to jam it in there.

The star of this story is the mouse. The forest in the story has plenty of redwood trees with their teeny, tiny seeds that sometimes take root and grow a two-hundred-foot-tall tree. But mostly redwoods reproduce asexually, which makes some kids laugh, but it's not funny when you use the word asexual in a science-class kind of way. Look it up in the dictionary.

The other main tree in the forest is called the Douglas Fir, or Doug for short. Whoooo, Nelly! It hurts your neck to try and see to the very top. It doesn't have fur, like you might think from the name. Like every other tree, it has bark. Doug's cones are bigger than the redwood's and egg-shaped.

At the start of this story, Mr. Cator says that the Doug cones were nothing to write home about. I told him that this didn't make much sense because there were no people around to do any kind of writing. Mr. Cator said to forget about the people and the writing and to picture a big storm. The storm of the century! All the animals go running for cover. There are caves for the big ones, and earwigs can squeeze in anywhere, so they're safe. The only thing left out in the open is Mouse, who is freezing his fur off.

The kindhearted Doug tree notices and drops one of his egg-shaped cones by Mouse's feet. Maybe Mouse is a little ADHD because he doesn't get it at first, not until Doug issues a special invitation and tells Mouse to hop into the cone. He does. The cone keeps him warm and safe. In fact, when the storm is over, he decides to make the cone his permanent home.

So, whenever you're in the forest, it's easy to recognize. You can impress your friends with your astounding genius tree knowledge. It's the only cone that looks like it has the back end of a little mouse sticking out.

The end!!

seventeen

"This is wonderful. Wonderful!" said Mr. Cator. "What a bang-up of a turnout! So many eager beavers for our Nature and Ecology Club."

Honeysuckle folded her hands and looked attentive, even though I knew this was the last place she wanted to be. Charlie had a finger up his nose. Lupe was twisting her nose ring and sucking on a strand of hair. There were also some fifth-grade fosters, who looked worried.

How did I get them to attend? Did I punch or scream? Did I take anything that didn't belong to me and refuse to give it back until they bent to my will? No! I used my words. I blackmailed them. I took each kid aside and personally promised that if they didn't show up, they would never, ever in a million years make Termite's Top Ten popularity list. They wouldn't even crack the top thirty. Of course, Josh was there too. He came of his own free will and was sitting half in and half out of his box.

No person in his right mind would ever call this group "eager beavers," unless he was a liar or one of those peppy science teachers like Mr. Cator. Usually I don't like people who try so hard. Being around them is middle-evil torture.

"Medieval," Honeysuckle whispered back when I mentioned it.

"Middle-evil. That's the torture somewhere between not-so-bad and really bad torture." Mr. Cator's peppiness was demented, but in a good way. He took his job of official faculty advisor very seriously. He began, "The first order of business—"

"Snacks!" Lupe shouted. "Termite promised."

"Raise your hand and wait to be recognized," Mr. Cator said, which she did, and he said, "Lupe?"

"Order snacks!"

As the unofficial vote taker, I said, "All in favor of snacks at our next meeting, say eye."

Lots of eyes.

"Neigh?" I asked.

There were no neighs, so in big chalk letters, Mr. Cator wrote SNACKS on the blackboard. But before he finished the second S, someone asked, "What kind of snacks? Cookies?"

"No. Popcorn!" said someone else, then Charlie said, "Both! And maybe pizza."

I had to step in, or we'd be here all day thinking about ways to stuff our faces. Plus, it was a good chance to use the word I had just learned. Teachers always say to use a new word to make sure it sinks in. You should immediately use it five times in one day. "People! Do we want a nature club or a vomitorium?" That was one use.

"What's a vomitorium?" someone said.

"I'm glad you asked. A vomitorium is—" Two times.

Mr. Cator interrupted. "Is a word you can look up in the dictionary at another time. Let's focus on the matter at hand."

On the board, he wrote MASCOT and said, "We are officially open for nominations."

"A flying pig," suggested Charlie.

"Do pigs fly?" one of the fifth-graders asked.

Mr. Cator wrote FLYING PIG on the blackboard.

"That's dumb," said Lupe. "How about a bird?"

When Mr. Cator asked her what kind of bird, she looked puzzled and said, "You know, one of those *bird* birds."

"That's a vomitive idea!" I said. Three times.

Mr. Cator wrote it down anyway, along with all the other nominees.

3. DANCING COCKROACH
4. RUDOLPH
5. CUTE, FLUFFY BUNNY RABBIT
6. ELEPHANT

Arms shot into the air with more idiot suggestions. I ran my fingernails down the blackboard to get their attention. "Come on, people. There's only one real choice!"

"Not a pill bug," Honeysuckle insisted.

Mr. Cator wrote: 7. PILL BUG

"The banana slug!" I said.

Honeysuckle made a face. "Not that slimy thing!" and others joined in with "gross," "yuck," "no way," and "blah!"

"Fellow members, judge for yourself," I said. "Which sounds better? Go, dancing cockroaches! Or go, slugs!"

Lupe, who had nominated cute, fluffy bunny rabbit, kept accusing me of trying to jig the election.

"I'm not jigging it," I insisted.

"Rigging it," Honeysuckle corrected.

"That either!" I jumped out of my chair and invented a banana slug cheer right on the spot.

Oooooze to the left

Sliiiime to the right

Banana slug, nature girl, you eat vomitus all right.

Gooooooo, slugs!

Vomitus. That made four times.

"You can't have a cheer with vomitus in it," Lupe protested.

"Why not?"

"You can't have *right* rhyming with *right*. That's not right," Honeysuckle pointed out.

"Nature girl? Are all banana slugs girls?" Charlie asked.

"Actually, a single slug can be both," Mr. Cator explained.

"Both?" Charlie blurted out.

"Let's save the hermaphrodite nature of the slug for another time. It will make an intriguing meeting."

"Both?" Charlie was asking everyone around him. *"Both?"*

Mr. Cator looked weary. "Perhaps we should put the mascot question aside for another meeting. If Ms. Termite has concluded her spontaneous act of rambunctiousness, we can move onto the next order of business which is—"

The next order of business was put on hold because there was a tapping at the door and then a head sticking into the room. Mr. Cator glanced over his shoulder and raised one eyebrow before saying, "Striker, thank you for the honor of your company."

Striker! What was he doing here? He didn't say anything, not with his mouth anyway. His eyes did the talking, and they glared at anyone who looked his way. He took a seat way in the back of the room, which made Josh so nervous that he scooted into his box. Everyone else got quiet too. The number-one kid on the popularity list can do that. You let one in a room and suddenly everything you do or say feels like it is unbelievably stooopid with three Os.

But it was also torture for Striker being with us. I

could tell. His eyes kept darting back and forth to the window, like he wanted to escape.

◇

A bunch of us were taking a club break at the water fountain. "What's he doing here anyway?" Connie, the fifth-grader, asked. "Local kids don't join an ecology club."

"Striker's different," I said.

"Different from us, that's for sure," Charlie said.

"That's not what I mean. He's not just a whack 'em stack 'em kid."

"He's a spy," Lupe decided. "He's writing down all our names and is going to turn them over to his friends, and one by one, each of us will disappear and—"

"No," I insisted. "He really likes the forest."

Honeysuckle was looking at me funny. "When did you and Striker get so buddy-buddy?"

"We're not buddy-buddy. It's just that—"

Lupe made kissing sounds, and I pressed my hand over her mouth. What was I doing? Defending Striker? Why? Why did I care what the other fosters thought about him? He wouldn't stick up for me, not in a million years. "You're right. We have to watch him carefully. We can't let him get control of the club."

◇

That afternoon, we all voted our arms off, except Striker, who sat in the back of the room, acting like he was somewhere else. Soon we kind of forgot that he was even there. That first meeting, we got a lot of club business taken care of.

1. CLUB COLORS: mustard yellow and red, in honor of the banana slug and the redwood trees.
2. CLUB MOTTO: "Take nothing out of the forest except pictures and memories." Mr. Cator made us add "There's a special exception for teachers, who in the name of scientific inquiry may continue collecting unusual specimens that reveal the splendid possibilities of Mother Nature's trick versatility."
3. CLUB PROJECT: I volunteered to get all the information about the Adopt A Highway program and report back at the next meeting.
4. CLUB NO-NOS: Honeysuckle said that psychologists say people follow rules better when they are presented positively rather than negatively, so we came up with the following list of Club Yes-Yeses:

   Yes to treating the forest with respect.
   Yes to cleaning up after ourselves.

Yes to no torturing banana slugs and small insects.

"Not even ants?" Charlie asked.

"Not even," Lupe answered.

"What about club officers?" Mr. Cator suggested. "You can't have a club without elected leadership."

Everyone knows that school elections are basically popularity contests, and no one there, except me and Honeysuckle, had come anywhere near breaking into the Top Ten. So this would be an election actually based on the best kid for the job. Honeysuckle was a natural-born treasurer. I nominated her, "Because she's got a motto—waist not . . . what's your motto again?"

"Want not," she said.

"Yeah, she'll watch our money like it's tied to her waist and it would take aliens with mind-control devices to get it away from her."

The vote for Honeysuckle was unanimous.

Lupe nominated Josh for secretary. "He's back there anyway eavesdropping all the time. He might as well be taking notes." Everyone said "eye."

Connie won snack coordinator because her foster parents own Edna's Tree Hut. Another fifth-grader was elected "library chief of the nature guidebooks."

"Now for the important position of president," Mr.

Cator said. "We need someone who shows leadership ability."

I added, "And someone who knows the—what does the president need to know?"

"The ropes," Honeysuckle said.

"The ropes. Yes," Mr. Cator agreed. "This means that the president should have a great feeling for our natural environment. I would like to nominate—"

I started to stand.

"—Striker."

All heads swiveled. Striker's hands were up on either side of his face, palms and eyes spread wide, his head going no, no, no. Mr. Cator pretended to be blind.

"No, no," Striker said. "You promised that if I showed up today and didn't like it, I didn't have to come back. I don't want to."

Now Mr. Cator pretended to be deaf. On the blackboard, he wrote STRIKER.

A couple of kids groaned. Lupe put her head down on her folded arms. Everyone was disappointed because here was the chance for one of us fosters to finally be president of something, and Mr. Cator went ahead and destroyed that hope. I was more than disappointed, I was spitting mad.

Did I cough up a big ball of green phlegm and spit it in someone's face? No! I used my words and nominated

someone else. I nominated me. Charlie quickly sec-
onded it and started a chant: "Termite for Prez! Vote for
Termite!"

By the sound of it, I was going to win. I was definitely
going to clobber Striker. Man-oh-man, he didn't even
want to be in a club full of fosters, let alone president of
it. An *ecology* club. A club that was probably going to
vote to recycle! I bet even Striker was going to vote for
me. I would win. Hands down!

That is, if Mr. Cator hadn't come up with a plan.

"Two presidents," he insisted and gave us a look that
nobody, except me, dared to argue with.

"That's lame. Not even the United States has two
presidents!"

"That's a good point," he said. "What about a regular
president and a sergeant-at-arms president?"

Sergeant-at-arms. I had to admit that I liked the way
that sounded. I wasn't sure exactly what the sergeant-at-
arms president had to do, but it must have some kind of
uniform attached to it. *Termite, the mighty sergeant-at-
arms, looking crisp as toast . . .*" That was the job for
me. I had to have it.

"I accept," I announced and applauded as Mr. Cator
wrote my name next to Striker's.

That gave me a funny feeling, seeing our names up
there on the blackboard together. I looked around the

room, but no one else, not even Lupe, seemed to notice. In my mind, I put a plus between the names. Then, I started imagining a shape around them. It wasn't a heart shape. It wasn't! *Don't go there, Termite. Don't!*

"Termite? Termite! Earth to Termite." It was Mr. Cator calling on me to perform my first duty. I saluted him, then I saluted Striker, which made him sink even deeper into his seat. Then I proclaimed, "First meeting of the Forest Glen After-school Nature and Ecology Club is now adjourned. Everyone get out of here."

All in all, it was a successful meeting, even though I only got in four practices of my new word.

eighteen

Around sunset that same day, Striker and I wound up talking outside of the house. There was a heavy mist falling. Or maybe it was a light rain. It was always one or the other around here. People say that there are three seasons in Forest Glen: July, August, and rain. Everyone must have athlete's foot up to their ankles.

I told Striker that of all the members of the Nature and Ecology Club, I was the only one who hadn't been incriminated by him.

"Intimidated," he said. "*Incriminated* means there's evidence that you're guilty of a crime."

"I mean *incriminated*. You made everyone feel guilty just for being alive."

"That's crazy talk, Termite. How did I do that?"

"You know it. I know it. You broke the seven-second rule."

"What's that?"

"Anyone who looks someone right in the eyes for seven seconds without saying anything—that's incriminating. I use it on social workers all the time. It makes them feel vomitory."

There, I did it. Five times!

"I didn't stare anyone down!"

"You're pretty good at it. You don't even blink."

I followed Striker around the back of the house, behind the huge pile of wood, past the shed of Paul Bunyan tools, and around the back of that. We arrived at a bunch of cages that were stacked on other cages. Crates and glass jars sat on old falling-apart planks of wood that had been turned into tables.

Here was Striker's collection of spiders that he had promised to give me a tour of, but I didn't really believe that he ever would. He hadn't exaggerated. There was a whole Discovery Channel spider special back there. Big brown spiders and small red ones and a midsized black one that was surrounded by thousands of baby spiders.

"Wow. Invasion of the poppy seeds," I said. Then, my eyes latched onto all the other things. "Spiders are only the tip of the ice cube."

"Iceberg," Striker said.

There was a banana slug living in an old goldfish bowl filled with chunks of lettuce, wet leaves, and cones, with a screen on top to prevent escape. Looking out of wire cages, there was a cross-eyed gray squirrel and a jackrabbit with a black tail that Striker said was named *Lepus californicus.*

I decided to call him Loopy, since Lupe (the girl) was a big fan of cute, fluffy bunnies. Striker also had a lizard (western fence) and a snake (California king) that was curled into a shape that looked like a cinnamon bun. He pointed to a small, hoppy bird in a cage. "That's a chestnut-backed—"

"Chickadee," I said.

"How did you know that?"

"Nature girl, remember?"

And a salamander and a newt and a mouse and a turtle. Oh, yeah, Sickmub showed up and tried licking my hand, even though I kept nudging him away with the toe of my shoe. Striker pretended he didn't care that his dog suddenly wanted to be my best friend. I don't know what was up with that dog. You'd think I was walking around with raw hamburger meat in my pocket, which I wasn't. I checked. The only things in there were sunflower seeds and a dirty sock.

"It's Noah's art back here," I said. "Look at all the colors on the livestock."

"Ark, not art. But I see what you mean."

"Check out the pattern on that snake. I think I see a

secret message in there. No, a woman's face. It's one of those optical intrusions."

"Illusions."

I bent down to press my nose against the mesh of the birdcage. When I stuck in my pinkie, Chickadee hopped backward. She wanted out. I could tell. Striker got down on one knee next to me and looked into the same cage. He was so close that I could feel his breath on my ear. That gave me another one of those funny feelings in my stomach I didn't like. Or maybe I did like it. Maybe I liked it a lot. I didn't know what I was feeling, so I punched him in the arm. He backed off.

"What was that for?"

"For . . . for . . . for putting Chickadee behind bars. She should be out climbing a redwood with all her friends. It's not right."

I thought, *Someone should do something about it! Termite. A fearless freedom fighter who swoops down in the middle of the night to free all the caged creatures.*

I whistled a chorus of "Born Free," which is a song from an old movie, and even though it's about lions and Striker didn't have any lions caged up right then, it made my point. It took him a minute to recognize the tune. He plugged his ears with his fingers. "Who ever told you that you can carry a tune? And don't even think about it!"

"Think about what?"

"About opening the cages."

"What are you, a mind reader?"

He snorted. "Fearless freedom fighter! You don't even realize that you do it. You mumble aloud when you plot."

"Maybe I will let them out. I haaate zoos! Hate with three *A*s."

"Me too."

"Yeah, right," I said sarcastically. "Then what's *this* all about?"

"It's true. I don't like putting animals in cages." Striker stood, brushed the dirt off his knees. "I don't like being caged up either. Houses and schools are just cages for humans. One day, I'm going to be living out there."

When I asked, "Out where?" Striker tilted his head at the woods. "Why should I work in an office or some store when I can be outside looking up at the sky?" He paused. "I'm going to live out there. Be part of it. I'm never going to be trapped by four walls. Out there is where I belong."

I wanted him to go on because this was important information he was handing me. I knew plenty about feeling trapped. I was always thinking about taking off and finding a place where I really belong. A place that I'm really part of. I had a zillion questions for him. "When you live out there, what will you eat? How will you keep the mountain lions from eating you? Where will you sleep? What about friends? What about Diane Reener? What about Sickmub? I mean Babe. Will he go too? What will Diane Reener think? How will you hide when the police come looking for you and try to take you back, which is what always happens to me when I blow out of a foster home? How will you survive?"

"Termite, you've run away and lived on the streets in a city. You've gone to live with people you never met before and changed schools a lot. I can't imagine doing that. You're a survivor. You'd have no problem living in the forest."

"Really?"

"Piece of cake."

"But there are some scary things in there. Plus, all those trees and paths, it's so complicated. How do you even know where you are?"

"I guess it does seem complicated when you don't know it real well." He was looking off into the distance, like he had lost his train of thought, but only for a moment. "For me, it's simple. The most simple place in the world. It always makes sense in there when it's not making sense anywhere else."

I swallowed hard. This was one of those times when somebody says something that is exactly what you've been thinking, only you didn't even know you were thinking it until someone else gave you the words for it. The quiet in the forest. The light. The way I felt welcomed there, like I'd never felt welcomed anywhere. How there was always room for everyone, for bugs and birds, for both Striker and me. I wanted to start screaming, "Me too! Me too! That's exactly how the forest makes me feel!"

So I did. And then I danced the hula-karate and the happy chicken because if Striker—who was a forest genius—said I could live out in the forest, then I could. Why not? I definitely could. Piece of cake! When the turnaround came and the social worker said that I had to move to a new foster home, I could tell her, "Bye-bye. I already have a new home!" *The Mighty Termite, neighbors with chickadee and banana slug and Striker.*

"Permanent address: fourth limb up the gigunda tree."

Striker's face broke into a grin. He started laughing at me, not in the bad way, but in the way that said we had a connection going here.

"You should do that a lot more often," I said.

"Do what?"

"Laugh. You're always so serious around me."

He looked embarrassed and tried to stop grinning, but he couldn't.

"I don't have a butt in my chin like your relatives, but we can both be loggers, right?"

Something happened then, some kind of switch clicked off. Serious Striker again. His voice dropped to a whisper. "No, not a logger. Not me."

"Sure a logger. Your mother said—"

"Not me!" He crossed his arms against his chest and kicked at the dirt. "It's not that there's anything wrong with being a logger. It's a lot of hard work and dangerous. My father . . ." His sentence trailed off.

"Is logging how your dad lost his finger?"

He nodded. "But I'm not scared of logging or anything like that. It's more like . . . more like . . . it's just that cutting down trees day after day, if I had to tear down the forest like that, there'd be too much wear and tear on who I am."

Striker's eyes dropped to his feet. He mumbled something else.

"What?"

"I never said any of that stuff out loud to anyone."

"What stuff?"

"About not wanting to be a logger."

"What about your friends? What about Diane Reener?"

"Naw, they wouldn't have a clue what I was talking about. They like hanging out in the woods, taking a slingshot and knocking cans off limbs, that kind of thing. But if I told them my plans, they'd think I was some kind of environmentalist. And I'm not! I'm definitely a logger kid and— You're not going to tell anyone, are you? You better not."

"Tell what?"

"That I don't want to be a logger."

I crossed my heart. He draped a sheet over the bird-cage to keep Chickadee warm for the night. "Another thing. Diane's not my girlfriend."

"Oh," I said.

My eyes dropped to my feet, and he looked at the sky. I walked over to the banana slug bowl, and Sickmub followed. Striker caught up with us and scratched him under the chin. Sickmub, not the slug. "So you agree," I said. "They should be!"

"Be what?"

"Set free! The caged animals."

"They will be someday. Right now, this is for their own good. Chickadee has a broken wing. She's safe here while she mends."

"What about Loopy?"

"Paw problem."

"The banana slug?"

"That's different. I'm studying his ways right now. I'll release him soon."

"What do you mean, *his ways?* He's a slug. He slimes."

"That's what you think before you really get to know him. You should understand that. You've been living with Ike Eisenhower, and he's got a whole complicated life, right?"

That question made me remember when Ike and I first hooked up. He was the size of a freckle, rather than the pea he is now. "Every once in a while, Ike gets too big for his . . . what's he get too big for?"

"His britches?"

"Pill bugs don't wear britches! Too big for his skin, and he slips it off and then—get this—he eats it! Gross!"

"It's not gross. He doesn't waste anything. It's like I said, nature doesn't make mistakes. Ike is one smart pill bug."

Nobody—nobody!—had ever had anything nice to say about Ike.

Striker continued, "Look closer." Together we bent over the slug bowl. "How many antennae do you see?"

"Four."

"The top pair is longer, and the slug's eyes are at the very top. The bottom tentacles are shorter. That's how they feel objects and smell their food."

"Like how we use our noses to tell when there are fresh-baked cookies around?" I lifted my nose into the air. "What else do you know about him?"

"He has a long foot."

"I don't see any toes."

"Most of the slug's body, except for the head, is one long foot that moves him around. He's in the class Gastropoda. That's a science term that means 'belly foot.' His genus name is *Ariolimax*."

Striker was not only a tree genius, but a slug genius

too. He taught me a lot that day, about how the banana slug has twenty thousand teeth and likes hanging out in dark, hidden spots, which is something I could definitely relate to. He has two kinds of slime, one for sliding and one for sticking.

Pretty soon, it was too dark to see much of anything. When we started back to the house, I asked a big question. "You know that gigunda tree?"

"What about it?"

"What's with all the candles and stuff?"

"I'm not saying that I know anything. But if I did, some things just aren't your business, Termite."

"Honeysuckle and I gave the tree a name. Big Daddy."

"That tree is the mother of the forest. It's the oldest around. A lot of the other trees sprouted from it."

"Guess it should be Big Momma, then."

"Guess so."

◇

Later that night, I got a flashlight and went back outside. I tried to sneak, but Sickmub wouldn't let me out alone. We walked a little ways from the house. When I turned and looked back, I noticed that there was a light coming from a bedroom and both Mr. and Mrs. McCrary were standing there, looking out. I ducked because I thought they were looking right at me. But then I noticed that their chins were tilted slightly up. They were look-ing further out into the distance, out toward the forest, even through it was too dark to see anything.

They weren't talking, just looking, like they were memorizing the exact location for the future. After a while, he looped his arm around her shoulder and she buried her head in his chest. It gave me a squirmy feel-ing seeing that, like I was spying, like they had just decided something important.

"But something sad too," I said to Sickmub.

After the McCrarys turned out their light, I got back to work. It didn't take me long to find what I was look-ing for. Actually, I have to give credit to the dog who led me right to one. I prodded it with a stick and scooped it up with a piece of paper. Then I placed it in an old pickle jar that I had washed out and filled with lettuce, dirt, and twigs.

On the porch, I switched off the flashlight. Enough moonlight got through the clouds so I could study my find. It was a good one, fat and a wet, buttery yellow. This was going to be the best science project ever. Even Striker was going to be impressed. I really wanted to impress him.

At least it would be better than my fourth grade science fair project. That one was called "Snail Flying Lessons." I still feel kind of bad about it. All the snails failed.

nineteen

Science Fair Project Journal Entry #1
Questions Only a Banana Slug Can Answer

1. Do slugs mind bad breath? Or do they prefer a fresh, pepperminty scent?
2. Does a slug have a major depressive episode when it sees another slug getting squished to death by somebody's big, fat shoe?
3. Can slugs climb trees?
4. Do slugs like music?
5. Do slugs fart?
6. How do momma slugs make sure that baby slugs don't get lost or squished?
7. Can slugs do any tricks?

That was a good night's work. My brain hurt from coming up with so many science questions and being so orderly. I was about to close the notebook when I remembered something Mr. Cator said. That proves he's a good teacher because once school is over, you can count on me not remembering a thing teachers say. But what Mr. Cator said was impossible to forget.

One banana slug can be both girl and boy.

That opened a whole new kettle of slugs. I added:

8. Is the top half of the slug girl and the bottom half boy? Or is the boy-girl split down the center? Or is the slug a boy one day and a girl the next day? How does it work?

After that, I tried introducing pill bug to banana slug, but Ike was being a real pill and rolled himself up into a ball. It's too bad that they didn't click right away. It must be harder for bugs and slugs than it is for people. It's not like they can have an interesting conversation.

The slug needed a name, but nothing brilliant popped into my mind. Before I went to sleep, I made sure No Name was moist. Striker said that slugs breathe through their skin and it's all over if they dry up. I assured Ike that he was still number-one pet. Then I remembered that this was No Name's first night in a new place and when I'm in a new foster home, I can't sleep without something familiar. So I slipped outside again and came back with a Douglas mouse cone and put it into his/her jar.

◇

"Go! Go! Go! Go! Go!"

From way up high where I was, they looked as small as dolls, even the Portapotties. Honeysuckle stared up with amazement. Josh pumped his fist in the air. Even Diarrhea stopped flirting with Striker to watch. They both tilted back their heads. Striker had his hands on his hips. Not that I was taking any special notice.

At the very top of the rope, there was a bell that I rang, and the sound bounced all over the gym. Then I scooted back down—the Human Belly Foot—about a hundred times faster than I had climbed up. And no rope burn.

"How do you do that?" Honeysuckle asked.

Diane scrunched up her nose. "She moves all spidery, like a daddy longlegs. Doesn't she, Striker?"

I noticed that he didn't answer her. He did give me a thumbs-up.

"Forty-six seconds," said Charlie, who was holding the stopwatch.

"That's the school record, right?" I asked. "Right? Right?"

"Good job, Termite," said the PE teacher. "And don't keep asking me about the record. I said I'll check, but I doubt very much if anyone has kept a school record for speed-climbing the rope."

"Then I just set it!" I said, and no one, not even the Portapotties, argued.

The school record and a thumbs-up from Striker. I had just made the number-seven spot on my Top Ten Popularity List.

◇

After school, we held the second meeting of the Nature and Ecology Club. I wasn't sure that Striker would actually show up. I thought that maybe his friends would talk him out of it. But there he was, standing in the front of the room and taking his duties as copresident very seriously.

"Treasurer's report?" he asked.

Honeysuckle straightened her back. "We have a clean balance sheet. Meaning zero."

Striker asked for questions, and when there were none, he said, "Old business?"

Secretary Josh looked like he might jump back inside his box when Striker pointed at him. His hands flipped through a notebook. He said something.

"Louder, please," Striker said, and Josh said, "Old business. Report on the Adopt A Highway program," which made me say "oops!"

"That's the number-nine foster parent complaint about me," I admitted. "I forget to do what I promised to do."

Mr. Cator came to the rescue. "I thought it was such a monumental and appropriate idea for this club that I tracked down the information myself. Here's what it entails."

All teachers live to make lists and charts, especially science teachers. Mr. Cator passed around a paper that spelled out everything we could possibly want to know about adopting a highway.

THE ADOPT A HIGHWAY FACT SHEET
Each year, participants pick up nearly 250,000 bags
of trash from roadways—enough bags to reach
from Bakersfield to Disneyland!
Participants can do one or all of the following:
—*Collect litter*
—*Clean graffiti*
—*Plant trees and wildflowers*
Participants must take safety measures and
NO HORSEPLAY.

When everyone had enough time to read it, the sergeant-at-arms president—that was me—called for a vote. There were no neighs. Mr. Cator said we could get started immediately. Tomorrow, Saturday, at 9 A.M., we would gather at Edna's Tree Hut and meet our new adopted highway.

◇

The school bus dropped us off. Maybe this time, since Striker and I had gotten more buddy-buddy, he would say that it was okay for me to tag along with him when he went into the forest. But he did the same as always, which was to point in the opposite direction and wait until I headed off toward the house. I heard him call Babe and give a whistle. Sickmub flew off the porch and went running past me.

Let the dog ignore me. Who cared if Striker didn't want me hanging around? I had more important things to do. Science was calling.

Science Fair Project Journal Entry #2

Question #1 for a banana slug: Do you mind bad breath? Or do you prefer a fresh, pepperminty scent?

Hypotenuse: In a hypotenuse, you don't just make a wild guess. It's supposed to be logical. So my first guess was that the banana slug would prefer the pepperminty breath because who in their right mind wouldn't? But then I decided

I was thinking like someone who watches lots of toothpaste commercials. What banana slug watches TV? And why would a banana slug care about kissable breath when a slug doesn't even have any lips?

Besides, the slug lives with dead leaves and rotty things, so isn't it more logical that he'd feel more at home with death breath? That's what I used to call the breath of foster mother number nine when she would eat onion and garlic for dinner and then the next morning drink coffee and, without brushing her teeth, stand over me yelling, "Get out of bed now, or I'm gonna drag you out by your nose hairs!!"

Procedure: First, I did a spectacular job of brushing my teeth with the most pepperminty toothpaste, which Mrs. McCrary told me that she got on special at the Dollar Store. Then, I bent over the slug and gave him a good whiff. He didn't move at all. I swear he didn't. Science teachers always say to double-check the results, so I breathed on him again. Same deal.

Then, before I went to bed, I took an onion, peeled it, and ate it like an apple. Mrs. McCrary was watching and was extremely impressed. She said that most kids can't even chop an onion without crying and that I had a very special talent. "That's nothing. Look at this," I said. I took five hunks of garlic and popped them in my mouth like they were jelly beans. Mrs. McCrary said that she was concerned that I wouldn't be able to sleep because I'd have wild onion-garlic dreams. She told me that if that happened, I could come wake her up and she'd give me some medicine for acid indigestion.

Man-oh-man, she was right about all the dreams that night. One in particular. I can write about it on another piece of paper so it doesn't screw up this report.

In the morning, I scarfed down half a cup of coffee that Mrs. McCrary brewed. Loggers like their coffee to look like mud, and I didn't even put any sugar or milk in it. Then I went up to the banana slug who had all his tentacles out. I leaned over and hit him with Death Breath like I was blowing out birthday candles.

The results: Here it is! With pepperminty breath, the banana slug didn't budge.

Now get this! I was right. With Death Breath, his antennae disappeared back into his head. That proves beyond a doubt that he felt at home, like he was saying to himself, That's a familiar wind blowing my way.

End of Report

twenty

Termite's Wild Onion and Garlic Dream

I was in the forest, sitting on the edge of a big rock. Below me was a creek, the water flowing over boulders and logs. I stared down, watching little fish and water striders. I just stared and stared, thinking nothing at all. My eyes latched onto an ant, and I followed that ant as it roamed the banks, up and down, around leaves, along a fallen log. I stayed with it for what felt like hours until a boot appeared. I tried warning the ant. I yelled and yelled, but it kept going. The ant crawled under the boot, just as the foot hit the ground. I was so stunned by the sudden death of that ant that I broke down sobbing.

When I woke, my pillow was wet, and it took me a while to remember where I was.

Saturday morning, Mr. McCrary volunteered to drive us to Edna's Tree Hut for the Adopt A Highway cleanup. Was he in a better mood! I wondered what kind of happy, uplifting dream he had had the night before. He was a whole new and improved version of himself. He didn't shuffle around in his bathrobe and slippers, but put on jeans, boots, and the kind of flannel shirt that everyone around here wore. I called it the Forest Glen official uniform, and I wore a flannel shirt too, Striker's hand-me-downs. They weren't so bad. After the shirts had been washed a couple of million times, they weren't stiff or scratchy. The flannel didn't smell like me yet; it still smelled like Striker, but I wasn't complaining. I've smelled a lot worse.

"Nice morning," Mr. McCrary said. Then, "Take a breath of that crisp, clean air." And "Think I *will* have another pancake." And "Young lady, call me Lyman. No, call me Big L. Everyone does."

I said, "Okay, but you're not so big. My seventh foster father, Big Bart, now that was big."

Mr. McCrary—Big L—asked a riddle. "Got a good one for you. What do you call a timber terrorist?"

You'd think Mrs. McCrary would have said something to her husband, like *What drug are* you *on?* But she acted like nothing had changed, and she doubled over with monkey-cackling, knee-slapping, nose-snorting laughter when he gave the punch line: "Osama Bin Loggin. Get it? A timber terrorist."

Mrs. McCrary was laughing the way people laugh when a joke isn't all that funny, but you really like the joke teller and want him to keep feeling good about himself. All this time, Striker's eyes were bouncing back and forth from his mother to his father. I was watching his mouth. A couple of times he started to say something. He was dying to say something. I sent out my most powerful mental gyrations trying to get him to ask what the heck was going on. But Striker kept quiet. Only when his father suggested that we leave a little early for Edna's and take the back route—"It's a little longer, but there's something I want you to see"—did Striker finally speak up. He said, "Er, um, yeah, sure. Of course. Of course!"

Big L gave us the okay to ride in the open bed of the pickup, so Striker and I hopped in. I kept asking, "What's going on? What?" and he kept saying, "Did you brush your teeth this morning? Your breath stinks," and I tried to tell him about my slug experiment, but soon the truck was going too fast and there was too much wind to say or smell anything.

We didn't get on the main highway, but stuck to little roads. We went up and up a bunch of winding gravel and dirt paths, like we were heading to the top of the world. The last road was so steep and bumpy that we had to hang on to the side of the truck. I was sure we were going to fall out and go tumbling down the hillside. Higher and higher we went, around and up, until we stopped at a pullout.

Big L bounced out of the driver's seat. He opened his arms like he couldn't get enough of the air and the trees. Striker and I trailed after him until the three of us were standing at the edge of a cliff. Big L was really on the edge. Inside his big, clunky logger boots, I bet that all of his toes were hanging over.

That reminded me of something Honeysuckle had warned. You really have to keep your eyes glued on people with major depressive episodes. Some of them, she said, like to take too many pills or jump off bridges. I was thinking, *Man-oh-man, I hope Big L didn't drive us all this way for **that***.

I *know* I didn't say that out loud, so I'm guessing that Striker was having the same creepy thought, because he inched really close to his father. He hooked his arm around his shoulder, which looked funny, since his father was two heads taller. It must have been uncomfortable. Striker tried his best to make it look like one of those friendly father-son moves. But I could tell it was really an I'm-not-about-to-let-you-sky-dive-without-a-parachute move.

It was a long way down there. Walls of trees rose up from all sides. I saw more shades of green than anyone had names for. We stood at the edge for a long time.

Big L didn't jump off. I guess I didn't really think he would.

"Keep your eyes open," he said. "Pay attention."

For a ball of energy like me, that's not the easiest thing in the world to do, especially when I don't know what I'm supposed to be paying attention to. I hummed a little. I tossed a small rock over the edge and lost track of it way before it hit bottom. *If* it hit bottom. Then I coughed up a ball of phlegm from the back of my throat and spit it over the edge. I thought about how it would feel if I jumped off. *Flying, turning triple-somersaults, flat on my back, arms folded behind my neck, la-la-la, hum-hum, more flippies. Never hitting bottom! The Amazing, the Mighty—*

"There! That's what we're waiting for!" Big L was pointing straight ahead. "Twelve o'clock."

I didn't get what he was saying because it couldn't have been more than eight-fifteen or eight-thirty, tops, but Striker explained, "Like the hands of a clock," and I looked in the same direction that he was. I squinted. I concentrated.

I still didn't see anything. And then I did.

It was a big bird. A very big bird that had just taken off from one side of the cliff and was making swoops and swirls and flapping through the canyon.

In the pocket of my flannel shirt, I always kept the list of birds that Mr. Cator had given me. I pulled it out and shook off some sunflower seed shells. It wasn't a Steller's jay, and for sure it wasn't a chickadee. That bird out there could probably eat a hundred chickadees.

Let's say that I did jump off, performed my triple-double spins, and only thought I was falling forever, but there was the bottom and I hit it. That bird is looking for someone like the former me. Yum, yum, a tasty treat. Think I'll call over a few friends and we can pick her bones clean, even if there's not much meat on her.

"Vulture," I said.

"Good guess, young lady. But it's not a vulture. That bird out there is a hunter, not a scavenger. Striker, recognize it?"

"Eagle," he answered.

"Wrong!" I said. "I've seen pictures. An eagle has a head like a golf ball."

Striker looked over my shoulder and pointed at the bird list. "You're thinking of a bald eagle. This one's a golden eagle, one of the biggest birds in the sky. Their wingspan is huge. Picture me going up for a jump shot. Right, Dad?"

"He fills the canyon with his power, don't you think?" Big L's hand was making an awning over his eyes. "But you didn't really answer my question, son. I know you knew it was an eagle. But do you recognize it?"

Striker, puzzled. "You mean, *that* bird? That particular bird?"

"It's been a long time since I took you up here. How can I expect you to remember? But that bird has been here as long as I have, as long as I've been a logger and even before that, when I was a logger's kid. My dad used to point him out to me and I pointed him out to you when you were younger. Eagles are like that. They find a place that feeds and protects and sustains them. Then they do whatever it is they have to do to stay."

The eagle landed on the highest branch of the tallest tree. He looked out over the canyon like he was king of it. "He looks kind of lonely out there all by himself," I said.

Big L turned and walked back toward the truck. "Alone," he said. "But not lonely."

twenty-one

Big L dropped us off and we joined the other members of the Nature and Ecology Club, who were gathered outside of Edna's Tree Hut. Mr. Cator checked off our names on his clipboard. Honeysuckle linked arms with Josh, who was clearly scared out of his socks to be out in the open. Their heads were close together, and she kept whispering peppy you-can-do-it things to him. So far, it looked like her psychology was working.

Charlie and Lupe were both eating. "Take a bite," she offered, and I did. "It's the special. Spotted fowl burger. With ketchup."

"Hmmm. Spotted fowl. Good. Tastes like chicken."

"It *is* chicken," Mr. Cator said.

From the far side of the parking lot, two boys carried a couple of cardboard boxes that they had taken out of the back of Mr. Cator's truck. One of the boys was Striker, and I kept sneaking peeks at him. I don't know why, but I couldn't stop myself. I wondered if he wanted to talk to me the way I wanted to talk to him about the eagle his father had shown us. When he saw me looking his way, his eyes got wide, surprised. But I think he also looked pleased. I swear he did, at least a little, because he let his eyes linger on mine for a second before we both looked away.

The front door of the restaurant opened. Connie and a skinny man wearing an apron hauled over another big box, which was filled with bagged lunches. There was one for everyone except for the two that Lupe and Charlie had already scarfed down.

Mr. Cator made a big production over the fact that the lunches had been generously donated by Barton Taylor, who was the owner of Edna's, along with being Connie's foster father. Everyone applauded. You could tell Mr. Taylor and Connie liked each other. The happy looks they exchanged weren't something you could fake. Then Mr. Taylor held up one of the bags. "I packed each of you our daily special sandwich, which includes a bag of chips, a soda, and one of the oatmeal chocolate chip cookies from the new Edna's Cookie Company that my wife, Doreen, is trying to get up and running. Connie here has been a big help. No charge for any of this."

More applause led by Mr. Cator.

I jumped up and down with my hand in the air. "Question! Question!"

Mr. Taylor pointed. "Okay. You, the shrimpy-looking girl."

"Who's Edna?"

"Edna was my grandmother, long in the ground. She started this restaurant. Look at the sign by the entrance there. Established in 1931." Mr. Taylor coughed into his fist to clear his throat. "That leads me to something that I want to make clear. I'm pleased to be supporting you on the nature part of your club, cleaning up the highway and such. But as I told Connie here, I feel a whole lot different about the other part. The E word—and I don't mean Edna—doesn't sit too well. A lot of you are new here, but the families that took you in feel the same as me and I know that—"

Mr. Taylor was on a roll, and I started getting antsy. Lupe was digging into her chips. Mr. Cator kept looking at his watch. That's when a big car made a wide turn into the parking lot. The tires kicked up gravel. Music blared from the radio. A man with slicked-back hair and a really big smile rolled down the window and leaned out the driver's side.

I figured he was lost and asking for directions. The families around here drive banged-up trucks, not a shiny red car with a killer sound system. The man was a loud talker. "Not too late, are we? My little girl decided, yes, this is something she wants to do. She's civic-minded, like her old man."

The car door opened, then slammed close. Holding a picnic basket was Diane Reener. That was how I learned that she's the daughter of the vice president of the lumber company that had laid off three-quarters of the loggers in town.

"You got your cell phone, right, honey?" the man said. "You'll call when you need to be picked up?"

She ignored him. Her eyes scanned the group and got wide and bright when she found who she was looking for. Civic-minded? Diarrhea was Striker-minded!

She walked up to him, scrunched her nose, and looked into the cardboard box by his side. "Oh, look, Striker. Little orange worker safety vests. How cute! This is going to be so much fun."

In my head, I heard Striker's voice say, *Diane's not my girlfriend.* But seeing them in their matching orange vests? She wiped away his dirt mustache.

Who cared?

◇

Man-oh-man-oh-man! You can't believe the stuff that winds up on the side of a road. I knew there'd be soda cans, beer bottles, and gum wrappers. Hey, I probably once tossed an empty bag of sunflower seeds out of a car window myself.

Okay, maybe twice. But never again! Never will I litter! Not after spending hours picking up things that were plastic and grimy or metal and rusty or papery and moldy. And if you ever toss a half-eaten apple out the car window and think, *I'm not littering. That's all natural!* think again. Because someone has to pick up your brown, slimy, smelly half-eaten apple that's coated in cigarette ash.

"This is nasty!" said Diane, who was holding up a stretched-out sock with green and brown stains. Nobody wanted to think about what made those stains. After that sock, Diane officially quit for the day. I figured that Striker was going to join her, the way she started flipping her hair in his face and pulling on his arm. I saw them talking for a while, but he shook his head firmly, and her mouth dropped open. She couldn't believe it. Then she stomped off and sat under a tree, sulking, her arms against her chest.

After that, I was really struck by cleaning fever. Every time Striker and I crossed paths, I made sure that he would be impressed. I held up a half-eaten fried chicken carcass, and he gave me a big thumbs-up, which was pretty funny because we were both wearing big black gloves that made our hands look swollen to five times their size.

"Adopting a highway is hard," I said to him. "This is the grossest day of work I ever put in."

"Me too," he agreed. "But what's the other choice? You can't just give up."

"Right," I said. That seemed really lame, so I said, "Exactly." But that still felt pathetic and not enough, so I said, "Give up? Man-oh-man, you can't just turn your back on something you've decided to adopt."

Striker lifted his safety goggles. Right while he was looking at me, his eyes morphed into his father's eyes, same flecks, same stubbornness. He took a deep breath and from the slow way that he let out the air, I could tell that I—who was always saying the wrong thing—had said exactly what he wanted to hear.

◇

Science teachers are big fans of lists, so Mr. Cator asked Secretary Josh to write down everything that we saw that didn't belong on our adopted highway. Along with the disgusting sock and fried chicken carcass, we found

1. cigarette butts
2. empty packs of cigarettes
3. running shoe with no shoelace, size 8
4. gnawed BBQ rib bones
5. pillows with feathers sticking out

6. baby's pacifier, blue
7. cartons for fast-food hamburgers
8. empty cans of soda
9. pieces of newspapers from 2001, 2003, and the day before yesterday
10. old Superman comic, ripped
11. the top of a girl's bathing suit
12. broken pens
13. a cardboard box of empty motor oil cans
14. coffee cups stolen from Edna's, both chipped
15. red shotgun cartridges from hunters
16. entire couch with springs sticking out

We filled eleven garbage bags with trash, and I helped drag them to Mr. Cator's truck so he could drive them to the dump. No way would they stretch to Disneyland, but it was a start. It took four kids to drag the couch.

◇

Striker and I got an idea for our own list. We wrote down all the things that we saw that *did* belong there. My handwriting stinks, so Striker wrote. I yelled:

1. Douglas fir and cones
2. redwoods
3. chestnut-backed chickadee
4. red-tailed hawk on telephone pole

5. brush rabbits
6. black-tailed deer poop
7. buckeye trees
8. manzanita shrubs
9. mosquitoes
10. banana slugs

We weren't sure which was the right list for the dead salamander with its eyes popped and guts hanging out in the middle of the road. I didn't want to just dump it into a bag of cigarette butts and chicken bones, so a few of us decided to bury it. We pushed past the manzanita brush, until we were well off the highway.

I dug a small hole. We formed a circle. I had to force Charlie and Striker to hold hands, but they did it. "Okay, I'll start," I said. I lowered my head. "Salamander, sorry you got smashed to smithereens by a big rig." I turned to Josh, who said, "Do I have to?" and when I nodded yes, he said in a rush, "I never got to meet you personally, but I bet you were a fine salamander."

Charlie shook his head no, and so did Striker, but Lupe said, "Me next." She bowed her head. "Salamander, maybe you didn't have the good luck to be born with fur. Maybe you weren't soft and fluffy in this life, but in your next life, maybe—"

"Okay, that's good," I said. Enough was enough.

All and all, it was a good day. We had spotted fowl

burgers. We had a funeral. Our adopted highway was clean as a whistle, even though I don't know any whistles that are clean because people spit in them. Josh didn't duck off and hide somewhere. There were no fights. Mr. Cator found some interesting specimens of something right off the highway. Honeysuckle found seventy-nine cents in pennies and nickels. Even the weather was better than the usual drip-drip-drip.

At three o'clock, Big L picked us up, and he was still in a good mood. He stayed that way all through dinner.

◇

"It's a record," I told Honeysuckle over the phone that night. "He's cracking jokes. He's a regular high-fiver."

"Live wire?" she asked.

"That too."

"Same here. My foster parents aren't even home tonight. They're out to dinner. They never go out to dinner. They always say they don't have money for such luxuries."

"Things are looking up in Forest Glen," I said.

Silence from Honeysuckle's end, then, "My foster mom wants to take me shopping to get new clothes."

"New? Not hand-me-downs?"

"See what I mean? It's making me nervous."

"Honeysuckle, everything makes you nervous!"

"I don't think I'm imagining this. Everyone seems happy, but happy worries me."

"Ah, that's just a typical foster-kid thing to think. When things get too good, fosters get suspicious. I do. I start thinking, Good doesn't feel right. Good doesn't last."

"Hmmm. You have a point. Maybe it's just me, an example of negative thinking." Pause. "No, that's not it. I'm not imagining it. Charlie says his foster parents are acting like it's Christmas. Lupe says that her foster father is humming show tunes from *The Sound of Music.* Something's going on."

I had an idea. "If everyone got depressed at the same time, can't they—presto-chango—get undepressed at the same time?"

I heard her flipping through her psychology book. "Okay, here it is. It does say that depressions can suddenly lift."

"See, I told you! Just like that." I snapped my fingers.

"Wait, there's more. It also says that it can be a sign of mass delusion."

"What's that?"

"It means that everyone—your foster family, mine, probably the whole town—may be living under the illusion of false hope."

twenty-two

Word had gotten out that Striker was president of the Nature and Ecology Club and that we had gotten free food. Suddenly, it was *the* place to be. At the next meeting, even the Portapotties showed up. Striker called for the treasurer's report (still a big, fat zero) and old business (none).

Mr. Cator went first with new business. In front of the room, there was an easel with a sheet draped over it. "A little fanfare music, please, Termite," so I hummed "ta-da-di-da," and with a dramatic flick of his wrist, Mr. Cator revealed a sign:

ADOPT A HIGHWAY PROGRAM
This section of highway courtesy of
The Forest Glen
After-school Nature
and Ecology Club

"Whooo, whooo, whoooo!" Charlie started chanting. A lot of us joined in stamping our feet and clapping hands. We kept it up for a while. I did notice that the Portapotties, who usually never miss a chance to get rowdy, were way too quiet. They scowled. Diane said something to Connie, who immediately stopped clapping. Pretty soon it was only me and Charlie who were keeping up the cheer.

Portapotty #2 left his seat and whispered something to Striker, who nodded, then called for silence. "Are there any comments concerning the new highway sign?"

"We don't like it," said Portapotty #1. "We've got a problem with the E word. What about calling it the Lumber Lovers Club? Or the Timberjacks. That E word really sticks in our . . . in our . . ." He looked around for help.

"Craw!" I said. "But this isn't even your club."

"It's a free country. We want to join." He looked around at his friends. "Don't we?"

The Portapotties drew themselves up taller. I drew myself up taller, which wasn't very tall. From the back of the room came a voice. "Josh has an idea," Honeysuckle said. "Go ahead, Josh."

"He speaks?" Portapotty #1 said. "The kid in the box speaks?"

Honeysuckle had to give Josh a little push in the small of his back to get him moving. He took a few steps forward, then a few more. He walked like he was on a tightrope and there were bears to the right, lions to the left, and a forest of stinging nettle below. When he reached the front of the classroom, he asked Mr. Cator for a marker and drew lines through the words *Nature and Ecology Club.*

The Portapotties slapped palms. A group of fifth-graders gave a disappointed "awwwwww."

In its place, Josh wrote the word SLUG, so the sign read: "This section of highway courtesy of the Forest Glen After-school Slugs."

Portapotty #1 groaned. "No way. Sounds like a bunch of losers."

"It's got no spirit," #2 agreed.

"I'm not an after-school slug," Connie protested. "I help out at Edna's. I wash dishes, and I'm learning to work the register."

"Sorry, Josh, but slugs *are* sluggish," said Lupe.

"And yellow. Like cowards," said Charlie.

Another popular kid stood. "They don't have any spine. You taught us that, Mr. Cator. They're spineless."

"Like I said, cowardly," Charlie repeated.

Nobody had anything nice to say and nobody waited to be called on.

"Slugs are both boy and girl. What kind of club is associated with *that*!"

"We all know what they eat!"

"What *do* they eat?"

Diane whispered into a girl's ear, and the girl put her hands over her mouth: "Gross! They eat vomitus!"

"Slugs eat redwood saplings," Portapotty #2 said. "They can chew down the whole forest. My dad says—"

"Your dad's wrong."

Portapotty #2 narrowed his eyes and looked around to see who had the guts—and the stupidity—to criticize his dad.

Man-oh-man, it was Striker, and he said it again. "Your dad's wrong." His chin with the family hole in it was jutted forward. He started defending the slug, like it was a member of his family that had been insulted. Like the slug was his clumsy, funny-looking little brother who everyone made fun of but was really a great kid if you gave him a chance.

"Banana slugs don't eat redwood saplings," he insisted. "They'll starve to death before they'll touch a redwood."

"That's not what my dad says. He says—"

"Hopper, no disrespect to your dad meant, but he's dead wrong about the banana slug. I tested this myself."

We looked to Mr. Cator for the final word. "It does makes sense. The slug avoids the small redwoods, which helps maintain the foggy, damp habitat that they need for survival. Perfect scientific sense!"

"I know something else. They have twenty thousand teeth," I said.

Diane gave me a disgusted look. "Termite, shut up. They don't have teeth."

"They do!" Striker and Mr. Cator said together. The teacher made a big, showy bow to Striker, who continued. "Termite's right. They have a tongue called a radula, which is covered with lots of rows of tiny teeth. To eat, they scrape against everything in the forest, all the debris and living things, except the young redwoods."

"You might say that the banana slug is the cleanup and recycle crew of the forest," Mr. Cator added. "Plus it's native to our community. Seems to me that it makes the perfect mascot."

"But they're so sluggish," someone pointed out. "It'll sound like we hardly work."

"The fastest ones can go point-zero-two-five miles per hour," Striker said. "That's like you going twenty-six feet in one minute. Try doing *that* flat on your belly."

I did. I was the only one. I plopped on the floor. "You can't use hands or knees. The belly always has to be touching the floor." I scooted toes, then butt, moving my body like a wave. I didn't get very far. "This is harder than it looks."

"Now, Striker," Diane said, "I know the slug has some

good traits, but all that mucus! Yuck! Nobody thinks well of mucus."

"That *yuck* is a human attitude problem," said Mr. Cator.

"Two kinds of mucus!" I yelled from the floor. "Sliding mucus and the sticking kind." I jumped up and brushed off the dust, pencil shavings, someone's not-so-old gum, the *debris* of the classroom.

The slug's bright yellow problem didn't turn out to be a problem at all. Everyone, even the Portapotties, admitted that it was a great color, very unique. Honeysuckle pointed out, "I know that *yellow* is a synonym for *cowardly,* but psychologically, cowards try hard to blend into the background. Yellow really sticks out in the forest. The slug seems almost proud of it."

"Yeah," Charlie said. "Like it's saying, Just come and try to eat me. I'll give you a mouthful of slime!"

During the slug debate, Josh had been very quiet. Silently, he started writing something else on the Adopt A Highway sign. We couldn't see what it was because his back blocked the view. Finally, he finished and stepped off to the side.

The Portapotties looked at the sign, then at each other, stuck out their bottom lips, and gave their heads a serious nod. They approved. Mr. Cator laughed out loud. When Josh returned to the back of the room, Honeysuckle gave him a big hug.

After that, I called for a vote, and it was unanimous. Our new sign that would be on the highway for all to see:

ADOPT A HIGHWAY PROGRAM
This section of highway courtesy of
The Forest Glen School Banana Slugs

Both our mascot and my science fair slug needed names. Lupe tried to convince us to use the Spanish word for slug, which was *babosa,* but I have enough trouble with English. Honeysuckle suggested something psychological. "You heard what people think of the slug. What about a name that would enhance its self-esteem?"

"Like what?"

"The slug lives on the ground, so what about the opposite? Up? High? How about Your Highness?"

I rolled my eyes.

"Maybe not that, but something elevated."

Honeysuckle asked Striker to write out the scientific name—*Ariolimax*—and the next day we considered the possibilities.

Max. It was simple and easy to remember. There was no one at the school named Max, not even a teacher. Besides, Max can be both a girl and boy name. That's important, considering the slug's nature.

I decided that the slug living in the pickle jar would be called Maxine.

We gave our mascot a name that would "boost" anyone's self-esteem. Maximum Max, or M-squared (M^2).

twenty-three

When I get to my next foster home and the kids there ask if I started to go nuts living in the middle of nowhere because there wasn't mini golf or a mall or even a middle school, I'll tell them my days were packed.

There was school and homework, of course, and the highway we adopted. Every other Saturday, we put on our Forest Glen M^2 Banana Slug sweatshirts and orange vests and spent the morning cleaning up.

Also, every day I had chores, like chopping wood and feeding Sickmub and taking Sickmub for walks because now he followed me everywhere. I don't know why because I wasn't always very nice to him—yelling at him to stop looking at me with his weird white eye and to not even think about sticking his nose in my crotch. Honeysuckle said that some animals can sense what people like and need, even when the person herself doesn't know it. Maybe Sickmub sensed that I kind of, sort of liked sticking my hand in his warm fur and giving him a big, rough belly rub.

There were other good things about Forest Glen that I never counted on. Having all these other fosters made it feel like I had a whole extra family in addition to the one I was living with. That was something. Two families, when most of my life I've had no family at all.

It wasn't like the McCrarys were a real family. I knew that I was a short-timer. But this "home" was better than most, especially now that Mr. McCrary was whistling and telling jokes and Mrs. McCrary was teaching me to cook. She said that I was a natural at it, even if I wasn't very good at cleaning up the mess I made. In fact, I was very bad at cleaning up. Still, that made two new things that I was a natural at. "Something to be proud of," she said.

My science fair project also took up a lot of brain time. I was obsessed. Trust me, it's not easy to get a slug to cooperate. Honeysuckle, Charlie, Lupe, and Josh joined as co-scientists. So far, we had figured out the following:

Do banana slugs climb trees? Yes.

Can banana slugs do tricks? Yes. They can produce a strong see-through slime cord and lower themselves from a branch.

Do banana slugs fart? Answer still up in the air. (Up in the air, ha-ha-ha.)

Do banana slugs feel bad to find another slug that's been squished to death?

To answer this last one, we found a squashed slug and put it in the pickle jar with Maxine, who slithered over and around it.

"She doesn't seem to notice at all," Charlie said.

"But at least she's not eating it!" Lupe said.

Are banana slugs cannibals? Not Maxine!

◇

A couple of times a week after school, I followed the trail to the Big Momma tree. She was always there, surrounded by all her children trees. I got to know the Steller's jay that lived there, and he got to know me so well that he'd come and sit on a nearby stump. I didn't know you could click with a bird, but we did. I think it was because he was as noisy and hyper as me.

At this time of year, mushrooms were sprouting everywhere. They weren't the whitish gray umbrellas you see in the supermarket next to the bell peppers and cabbage. These were as orange as pumpkins or as red as tomatoes. Some looked like hats. Others were shaped like tiny eggs, golf balls, shingles on a house, starfish. I saw some yellow ones that Mr. Cator called witch's butter, because when they soaked up water, they spread out and looked like melting butter on a log.

He reminded me that a lot of them are poisonous. He could have saved his breath because I won't even eat store mushrooms, not even if they've been fried in butter and garlic. There are only two things in the world that I won't eat. Anchovies and mushrooms, and I would eat anchovies first.

Hold on! Add banana slugs to the list of things I won't eat. One day, Big L told me that when the Indians who used to live in the forest got really hungry, they washed slugs in vinegar to remove the slime and then, down the hatch. He personally had never tried it. Charlie is the only one of us who said he might eat one, if we paid him enough.

Whenever I visited Big Momma, there were always small but important voodoo differences under the tree. A new candle, a different feather. One time, there was a stack of rocks, one balanced on another in a way that made it look like art. Better than art! It was still creepy, but not as creepy as before. I figured that if there really was a psycho-killer-voodooist, something would have happened to me by now. I got the feeling that whoever—or whatever—wasn't so interested in me. Big Momma was getting the attention.

One day when Honeysuckle was with me, we spotted

a nest at the base of the tree. The wind had been wild the night before, and it had probably fallen out. We got down on our hands and knees and looked at the three cream-colored eggs inside. One was shattered, but the others seemed okay.

"Bad luck, buddies," Honeysuckle said. That's when the Steller's jay showed up, and I said to him, "Don't even think about it," because Striker told me that jays can be very aggressive and steal eggs from nests.

Honeysuckle blew on the eggs to keep them warm. "It's too bad. The nest should be back up there and protected." She pointed to Big Momma.

"I'll do it."

"No way. It's impossible."

"For a normal human being, impossible. But for the Mighty Termite? Possible!"

"It's way too high to jump to."

"Boost!" I ordered.

We tried, but the boost didn't bring me anywhere close. Honeysuckle wiped the dirt of my shoe from her hands. I walked around to the back of the tree. "Where there's a will, there's a . . . there's a . . . what is there?"

"A way," Honeysuckle said.

"I knew that! And here it is!"

A limb of a Douglas fir had snapped off and fallen. It must have happened a long time ago because the wood was flaky and cracked. Ferns and mushrooms were growing out of it. It wasn't any big deal to see broken limbs. They were all over the forest. Only when this one had fallen, part of it was stopped from hitting the ground. It slanted up from the forest floor and leaned on Big Momma.

I stepped onto the limb and bounced a little. It felt solid enough.

"You can't," Honeysuckle said. "You won't."

I took a few steps forward. "The Mighty Termite rises to the challenge! Hand me the nest."

"You'll fall! I know you will."

"Doesn't your psychology book say to be positive? What about my self-esteem? Hand me the nest."

She did, and I began inching forward. Was I scared? Of course I was scared, but I couldn't say that to Honeysuckle, especially after all my bragging. I reminded myself not to look down, because once you look down, it's all over. I took one step, then another. I didn't have any trouble at all. Except for that one part near the top of the limb where it was steeper and more slippery than I counted on and I stumbled. I screamed. The jay awked, and Honeysuckle shrieked, but I managed to collapse to my knees while holding the nest.

"Be careful!" she shouted, and as soon as my heart went back into my chest, I yelled, "Thanks for the advice! I was trying to fall."

I decided to crawl the rest of the way with the nest

balanced in my right hand. There was no shame in that. It was a lot more slanted than it had looked from the ground. When the limb ended, I was still nowhere near the first branch of the redwood, but there was a nook where the trees met. The nest would be safe there, and I was sure that the momma bird would be able to find the eggs.

"Good job!" Honeysuckle yelled. "Now come down."

I took a minute to gather my breath. That's when I spotted it. A rope. It was old and covered with dirt, but thick and solid, as far as I could tell. When I pulled, it didn't break or even give very much. I perched on the limb, held on to the rope with double fists and lifted my feet just a few inches. If my full weight broke it, I wanted to be close to something solid.

It didn't snap. I moved my hands up a few inches, then followed with legs and feet. Another movement, then another. *Don't think too much. It's the same as the rope in the gym.* I climbed and climbed and climbed, until I stopped thinking at all, until I was part of the rope and the rope was part of me.

The next thing I realized, there was a limb right above me. I had done it. I reached up and grabbed the branch, letting go of the rope and letting my feet dangle. Something sharp dug into my palms, and a twiggy thing hit me in the face, but I ignored them. I pumped my body forward. With elbows straight, I let my body swing backward, then snapped my elbows tight against my body. That movement lifted my chin above the branch. I hoisted myself up. One leg went over the branch and then the other. I had the perfect seat. The scent of the tree was so strong, I sneezed. I dug some bark out of my palms.

From below, I heard Honeysuckle's voice: "Termite? Termite? Where are you? I can't see you anymore. Tell me you're okay."

"It's amazing in here," I shouted back.

It was. There weren't just branches and bark, the way it looked from the ground. It was a whole world, like the entire forest had been squeezed into one place, and I was swallowed up into it. Bugs, birds, squirrels. I even spotted a salamander. And me, right in the heart of Big Momma.

I tilted back my head. No, I wasn't at the heart, not anywhere near it. This first branch was more like the anklebone. The heart would be higher up, much higher. From the center of the tree grew a series of thick branches. They were spaced evenly apart all the way to the top. Or at least as far as I could see. Some of the branches lined up like a ladder.

"Termite! Come on! It's getting dark! I'm scared. Termite!"

"Okay!"

I let my hips slide over the branch and held on with my hands, hanging like laundry. Then I wrapped my legs around the rope and shimmied back down until my feet reached the Douglas fir limb. A few more steps and I decided to jump. After being so high, it didn't seem very far.

It's a good thing a redwood forest floor has ten zillion years' worth of rotting things. That gives it plenty of bounce. When you hit bottom, you don't break an ankle, and your butt hardly hurts at all.

twenty-four

Honeysuckle was right. Something was definitely going on with the grown-ups in town. I tried to get Striker to tell me, but he swore that he didn't know anything either. There was so much whispering, which is something that I know a lot about. To start, there's the kind of whispering that's not worth getting tied up in knots about. For example, my seventh foster parents kept whispering about someone. Their heads would go together, and their mouths got tight and worried. It was driving me nuts. I kept making out words. *She. Weight loss. Low energy. Not the same person she used to be* . . . I spent a lot of time in closets spying on them. Then one night we were watching TV and their favorite game show came on and the wheel-spinner in a sparkly dress came onstage. That's when my foster parents started their worried whispering right in front of me. "See, she did lose weight! Do you think she's unhappy? Sick? Do you think she's got that anorexia?"

Those foster parents never worried about me like that.

I say kiss my butt to that kind of whispering.

What was going on between Mr. and Mrs. McCrary was different, serious. One afternoon, they called Striker for a talk. That's a giant step in whispering, when the kid gets dragged into it. They told him to take a seat in the living room.

I stationed myself at the dark bend on the stairs. Sickmub put his head on my lap. I couldn't make out all of the conversation but what I heard went like this.

Big L: "*Pss* . . . rumors for a while, but . . . *psss.*"

Mrs. McCrary: " . . . hear it from us instead of . . . *mumble-mumble.*"

Striker: "Which sections?"

Big L: "*mumble* . . . from the company standpoint . . ."

Mrs. M: "All the studies say—"

Striker: "The company studies!"

Big L: "You see the situation. *Psss.* Bite the hand that feeds you . . . *psss.*"

Striker: "Why not somewhere else?"

Big L: "That parcel makes sense to the company."

Mrs. M: "Son, it breaks my heart . . . *mumble.*"

Big L: "Pauline! . . . Coddling . . . almost a man . . . reality."

Mrs. M: "Striker?"

Silence.

Mrs. M again: "Striker?"

The front door opened, slammed closed.

Mrs. M: "Should I? Should we?"

Big L: "Let him go. He needs to work it out."

Mrs. M: "But I . . . *mumble.* He's only . . . *mumble.* It's his whole . . ."

◇

That night Striker didn't come home for dinner. It wasn't until way after dark, when everyone was in bed, that the front door opened and slammed closed. I couldn't sleep. *Rumors-sections-company-situation-eating-heart-reality-what? What? What?* Around and around the words went, like chipmunks chattering away in my head. I tried to get them to make a connection, but they wouldn't. I tiptoed downstairs. Striker was sitting on the couch, one hand on his forehead, the other buried deep into the fur around Sickmub's neck.

"What's going on?" I asked. "I better get some answers, or I'll never sleep again."

"I hate them," he said.

"Hate who?"

"Get out of here, Termite. This has nothing to do with you."

"What has nothing to do with me?"

"This! Forest Glen is just one more stop for you. It's my life."

I didn't know what he was talking about. But the way he said it made me feel like the ant that got crushed in my dream, a big boot coming down hard on me. How did he know what I felt about anything? About Forest Glen. About the way his dad talked to me like I counted for something and the way his mom said I made her laugh. About our plans—Striker's and mine—to live in the forest one day. To make the forest my home. Was that just another big, fat lie? He didn't know how I felt. He didn't! He wasn't me. He wasn't anything.

◆

The next day, the reason for the whispering was cleared up by a front-page article in the *Forest Glen Mercury News*. Most people in town called the paper the *Mercury Snooze* because not much newsworthy ever happened around here. My favorite part (besides the comics) was the crime blotter, which listed calls to the police. These were a riot when you were used to hearing big city news. Here's a typical item:

> **Monday, 8:17 P.M.:** A citizen called to report that an unfamiliar dog was walking south on N. Redwood Drive. Monday, 8:46 P.M. Same

citizen called to report that the same unfamil-
iar dog was now walking north on S. Redwood Drive.

Finally there was some real news. Everyone was talking
about it. Honeysuckle and I spread the Sunday *Snooze*
across my bed. One article took up most of the front
page.

THE HILLS ARE ALIVE WITH
THE SOUND OF CHAINSAWS
North Coast Timber Company
Gets OK to Resume Logging

BY C. S. KRIM, MERCURY NEWS STAFF WRITER

FOREST GLEN——Logging days are here again,
and the whole town is celebrating. The
county's largest employer, North Coast Timber Company, will begin full-scale logging
operations later this week. Rumors have
been around for a while, but the word is
finally out.

After several court battles and new environmental studies, the state and federal gov-
ernments have opened several parcels for
logging.

"We are hiring back each and every

person that we laid off 18 months ago—from bookkeepers to loggers to mill workers," says William J. Reener, company vice president. "The economic impact is going to be a plus for everyone in town, not just our employees. Get ready, shopkeepers and restaurant owners. Forest Glen is making a comeback. Go, Timberjacks!"

This reporter also contacted several environmental and antilogging groups. When told the good news, the spokesperson from the Love-A-Tree Foundation, who says that his name is Heartsong, was negative and whiny as usual.

"We'll be there to protest the destruction of beautiful living things," he said. "We invite any like-minded individuals to join us on Monday."

"No wonder everyone's in such a great mood," Honeysuckle said.

In one photograph, company VP William J. Reener—that was Diane's dad—was shaking hands with the president of the Lumberville County Board of Supervisors. That was Charlie's foster father. Another picture showed Connie's foster parents removing the Spotted Fowl Burger

Special sign from the window of Edna's. In another picture, two men wearing hard hats and built like Porta-potties were giving the thumbs-up signal.

Honeysuckle read the caption aloud. "The Hopper brothers are ready to whack 'em, stack 'em, rack 'em, and pack 'em."

There was also a chart about how much money the logging would bring into the county over the next few years and what it would mean for the average family, the school system, and businesses. It did sound like good news. No wonder Big L and everyone else were so charged up. They would all be getting their jobs back. Big L wouldn't have to move someplace else. Maybe more work meant that more families would move into Forest Glen and there'd be enough kids for a movie theater and mini golf. Maybe Forest Glen Middle School would be back in business.

So why was Striker in such a bad mood? What was his problem? "I think Striker is looking a gift horse . . . where aren't you supposed to look a gift horse?"

"In the mouth," Honeysuckle answered, then licked her finger to turn the page.

On page three of the *Snooze,* there was a map of Forest Glen with a thick black circle around one part of it. The title said "Location of Logging Parcel."

Some kids are really good at reading maps. These are

the same kids who can put things together by following printed instructions. They don't get messed up by inserting part B into part D and throw the whole thing across the room because pieces don't fit and pieces are missing. I can't follow instructions, and I can't read maps. Honeysuckle says that I stink at both because I'm not a *visual* learner. Not only can visual learners follow maps and printed instructions, but first thing every morning, they write a list of all the things they have to do and don't have to be told thirty times to do them. Grown-ups really, really, *really* like visual learners.

Honeysuckle was one of them. She bent over the map and talked it out to me. "Okay, here is Forest Glen Elementary, and here's the main road by Edna's, and here's where we buried the smashed salamander." Her finger was now on the circle of the map. She looked at it, then looked out my window, then looked at her finger again.

I'm not a visual learner, but I got this picture and I didn't like it. I didn't like it at all.

Honeysuckle pushed the newspaper onto the floor, flipped onto her back, and gave the ceiling a dirty look.

"Bad news," I announced.

"Me too," she said. "You first."

I pulled on an imaginary cord and went *"Eeeeeeeeeeeeeeeeee."*

"What's that?"

"The sound of chainsaws. There." I pointed out the bedroom window toward the forest. The forest I walked in almost every day. The forest where Big Momma lived. The forest that accepted me in the same way that it accepted everyone else.

Honeysuckle didn't say anything until I asked, "You have different bad news?" She nodded. "Remember the turnaround? If Forest Glen has logging, why do they need fosters?"

twenty-five

The next morning. Listening to Big L whistle "The Sound of Music" reminded me of how happy he was that he would be working again. Mrs. McCrary too. That was real nice to see. But it also meant the forest might be stripped of trees, and all us fosters would be sent away. Striker was right. This was a messssss with about six *S*s. I was caught between wanting something and not wanting the same thing, and it was making my head spin.

While Striker and I waited at the bus stop, I asked, "They're not really going to cut down the Big Momma tree, are they?"

He flipped up the collar of his jacket and didn't answer.

"They wouldn't do that. Nobody would do that."

"Termite, shut your trap."

"Oops! Forgot my lunch."

"Better hurry. You know the bus driver won't wait."

I ran until I was out of his sight, and then I walked and then I walked slower. I didn't forget my lunch. Actually, I did forget it, but on purpose. By the time I got back, the bus was long gone, just as I had planned. I didn't bring any lunch, but I brought along Ike Eisenhower and Maxine the slug, in separate jars, of course. I kept walking faster, past the bus stop, toward the woods. Sickmub, his big tail wagging, yapped as he ran by my side to meet up with the others.

◆

"We are going to get in sooooo much trouble," Honeysuckle said. "Sooooo with five Os."

"No way," I said.

"We're going to a logging protest. That's trouble."

Lupe was twirling her nose ring. "My foster parents are really happy about the logging. If they think I'm against it, they'll probably tell my social worker they don't want me around anymore."

"*Are* we against the logging?" Charlie asked. "I didn't know we're against it. I thought we were just cutting school for the day. That's why I'm here."

"Lupe's right," Honeysuckle said. "We shouldn't take sides."

"Forgetting something?" I asked. "If they have logging, why do they need foster kids?"

"I know," Honeysuckle admitted. "But if we keep our mouths shut and don't make any kind of fuss, maybe they'll let us stay, even if they don't need the money anymore. I don't know about anyone else, but I don't want to change foster homes again. I'm sick of it."

"Me neither," Connie said.

Josh poked a stick at a banana slug. "If they cut down all the trees, what happens to this slug?"

"That," said Honeysuckle, "is exactly the kind of question we shouldn't be asking out loud."

I started down the trail. The others looked at one another, and followed.

"No one's taking sides," I said. "Do you see a big protest? Do you hear a big protest?"

I made them stop and listen. All we heard was the *awk-awk* of the jays. "We're just going to check it out. We won't say a word."

"No involvement at all?" Honeysuckle said. "Promise?"

"Promise. No one will even know we were there."

◇

Heartsong—spokesperson for the Love-A-Tree Foundation—looked like a forest creature. His long hair hung around his face in fat, hairy sausages. His beard was thick and braided with beads. A few redwood twigs were trapped in it. He was wearing shorts and a tie-dyed shirt. I really liked his necklace, which looked like some kind of sacred animal tooth on a rope of leather.

Holding a microphone in front of him was a reporter lady I recognized from KLBV—TV 6 Lumberville. Her face looked like a paint-by-number picture. There was dark blue eye shadow slathered on her lids and bright stripes of red on her cheeks and lips. She was speaking into a microphone: " . . . standing in front of the one-hundred-fifty-foot-tall redwood that the Love-A-Tree Foundation is trying to prevent from being logged. Mr. Heartsong—"

"It's just Heartsong, no mister. As tree-savers, we choose names that reflect our intense and profound connection with the great Mother Earth."

"Yes, of course. Heartsong. So tell me, what are you attempting to accomplish here?"

"To stop murder! Look at Jerry. Isn't he a gorgeous fellow? Doesn't he deserve to live?"

"Jerry?"

"That's the name I've given him. When you adopt a tree to protect, you get to give him a name. Jerry honors the late, great Jerry Garcia of the Grateful Dead."

The cameraman motioned for the TV reporter to turn slightly and point to the tree. Heartburn, or whatever his name was, walked over and wrapped his tie-dyed arms around the bark. After the big hug, he pushed aside the voodoo candles, bones, rocks, and feathers, like they didn't count at all. He sat with his legs crossed and chanted something that sounded like "ooooo, maaaaa, Jerry."

This was too much. Who does he think he is? Jerry? Adopt? Maybe he likes the tree, but Striker and I love the tree. So does the voodooist with the candles. Heartburn can't just show up and adopt a tree that's already adopted!

My left leg started vibrating, and I guess that I was saying what I was thinking, building it into a fury. My fist tightened. Honeysuckle knew what that meant because she took hold of my arm and sunk her nails into it.

"Ouch. What are you doing?"

"Your promise," she hissed back. She was desperate. "No involvement."

I tried. I really tried, but I couldn't hold myself back. "Hold your . . . hold your . . ."

"Horses," Connie prompted.

"Yeah, horses," I shouted. "First of all, that tree's name isn't Jerry. And he's a she, the mother of this forest. A lot of the other trees are here because of her. That's why we call her Big Momma, and she doesn't need someone from the Land of Concrete changing her name and adopting her because she's already being watched out for. She's already got a . . . what's she got?"

I looked to Honeysuckle, who was shaking her head at me, giving up. "A guardian."

"Lots of guardians. Us!"

The TV lady rushed over and stuck the microphone in my face. "And you are?"

"Termite."

"Termite? Is that a name that shows your connection with the earth?"

"Naw, just my name."

"Unusual," said the reporter. "Doesn't a termite destroy wood?"

"Does it? A termite destroys wood? I never thought of that."

"The others with you are . . . ?"

I started to say Honeysuckle and Charlie, but Heartburn *did* have a good idea with the nature names, so I made things up on the spot. "Big Momma's guardians are Daddy Longlegs, Sparkle Web, Bee, Waterfall." I wasn't sure who was who, but they could work that out later. I also introduced Ike Eisenhower and Maxine the Slug. Sickmub barked, so I said, "And this is Sickmub. Some people call him Babe."

I knew I was supposed to stay neutral. I thought of how happy Mr. and Mrs. McCrary were about the logging. I was supposed to keep my mouth shut, but the words pushed themselves out. I leaned closer to the microphone. "It's more than us here today. Someone else adopted this tree too, only I don't know who it is, but someone's been holding a vitual for Big Momma, and whoever that is isn't going to let anyone hurt this tree because . . . well . . . we won't."

The TV lady motioned for the cameraman to move closer. When I looked into the lens, I could see my reflection, with Honeysuckle in the background. She had her face buried in her hands. Charlie kept waving and making weird mouth twists. Lupe fussed with her hair and nose ring. Josh was too short, so you could only see the top of his head. I could also see Big Momma in the background, which looked like it was growing out of my head.

"Termite, you're just a youngster. What are you, eight?" the TV lady asked.

"Eleven. I'm shrimpy."

"Why does an eleven-year-old want to save a tree?"

My mouth opened, and for once, I didn't blurt out the first thing that came to my mind. This was one of those questions that seems easy to answer at first. Because the tree is part of nature. Because the tree is older than just about anything else. Because, man-oh-man, where else would the banana slug live? Those were all good answers, but even taken together, they didn't add up to what I really wanted to say. *Why do I want to save the tree? Why?*

I walked over, leaned against the bark, felt the soft but scratchy texture on my skin. The bark was home to bugs and fungus. The branches were home to birds and lizards. And to Striker and to me. This tree had made it through droughts and storms, but now what was going to happen to it? "Just think about it, reporter lady," I finally said. "Most of the time, the mom protects the kids. But sometimes, the kids need to protect the Big Momma."

The reporter lady stepped in front of me and smiled at the camera. "From the mouths of babes. Well, folks, it looks like things are really heating up in this peaceful forest setting. We'll bring you more on this continuing controversy as the fight to save Big Momma unfolds. Reporting, this is Ana Guterson, KLBV News."

I had one more thing to say, so I kept jumping up behind Ana Guterson, my arms flailing in the air. I shouted, "Foster kids. Not just kids. Foster kids!"

◇

Cool banana slug trick number two: While I was talking to the reporter, I placed Maxine on the ground. When I looked, she was gone! She was even better at running away than I was. Her slime trail ran down the outside of the pickle jar. That's one of the benefits a slug has over a snail. When you don't carry your home on your back, it's a lot easier to slip in and out of places. I didn't feel too bad about Maxine taking off. This was where she belonged anyway.

◇

"We won't take sides? No one will even know we were there?" Honeysuckle hissed at me. "No one will even know we were there?"

The next morning on the school bus, she rattled the front section of the *Mercury Snooze* in my face. The headline read:

FOSTER KIDS ADOPT MOTHER OF THE FOREST
Termite's Band Vows to Save the Tree

There was a picture of me jumping with my arms raised. In another picture, Heartburn was meditating by the tree, and it looked like Sickmub was sniffing his crotch, but I know Sickmub was only licking his hand. In the biggest photo, Heartburn and I were doing some kind of super-secret Indian nature handshake of peace that he taught me. Heartburn actually turned out to be okay. When I said that I really liked his necklace, he gave it to me because he said we were siblings of the spirit. I don't know about that sibling stuff, but I liked wearing the necklace tucked into my flannel shirt.

"Don't be jealous!" I told Honeysuckle. "I'll let you wear the necklace sometimes too. Heartburn says—"

"Heartsong, not Heartburn! And that's not what I'm upset about. I grabbed the newspaper before my foster parents could see it. Last night was the worst. I exhausted myself keeping them away from the TV news."

"How'd you do that?"

"First, I pulled the plug and then—"

I tapped my index finger to my temple. "That's using your gourd. So what are you worried about? Your picture isn't in the paper. It doesn't mention your name. Nobody but us knows that you're Waterfall."

"Sparkle Web."

"Really? I pictured you more as Waterfall. So, who's Daddy Longlegs?"

"That's Char— Termite, don't change the subject."

"Relax. If anyone has to face the magic, it's me. But I got the newspaper problem solved."

"Face the music, and solved how?"

"It's all under control. I cut out the article and pictures. When the McCrarys open the newspaper this morning, the article will be missing. They can't get mad about what they can't see. Genius, right?"

twenty-six

Everyone had watched KLBV News. I couldn't go any-where in school without someone making a crack. In the hallways, half the kids I passed chanted, "Ooooo, maaaaa, Big Momma." The other half snarled, "Traitor."

Diane Reener was caught passing a note about me in history class. The teacher read it, shrugged, and handed it back to her. He didn't even make her throw it away or apologize. What kind of teacher is that? The note was a drawing of a banana slug body with my head. I have to admit that Diane is a pretty good artist. One arrow pointed to my dishrag hair, one to the big hole that the banana slug breathes through, another to the banana slug anus. I didn't have to look up that last word.

In the hallway, I tried not to walk between the Por-tapotties. I really tried. But they closed in on me like two pieces of doughy white bread. "Traitor sandwich," they said. The next thing I knew, I was jammed into a locker with the door slammed closed. I had to pound and scream bloody murder before Mr. Cator heard and let me out.

"You're doing a very, very brave thing, Termite," he said. "Brave, but true social suicide."

"Thanks, Mr. Cator. I have an important question for you about termites."

I asked him what I needed to know, and we went to his classroom. He showed me something in a book and then showed me a picture. That was my answer, and it was an answer I really liked, which made the day better for a while, until it was lunch period. I stood in the cafeteria line with an orange tray. The lady behind the counter said, "You're that Termite kid, right?" She didn't even wait for my answer. She dumped four heaping portions of lime Jell-O on my plate, even though she knows I hate lime Jell-O. She also said that they were out of French bread pizza when I could see four perfectly good pieces sitting right there.

The period before lunch, Honeysuckle had started moaning that she was sick to her stomach and called her foster mother to take her home. Lupe too. I'm sure there's something in the psychology book about *that*. For the first time in weeks, Josh spent lunch period in his box. When I took my tray to the leper table, the other foster kids got squirmy. "We're not mad at you or anything," Connie explained. "We just can't be associated with Termite's band." They moved to another table.

As far as I could tell, there was no one left on my side, not Striker, not even any of the other fosters. I said to my Jell-O, "Ready for this week's Top Ten popularity list? In the number–eighty-seven spot—out of eighty-seven—that would have to be me."

◆

I opened the front door and things looked *dum-de-dum-dum*. If school had been bad, this was going to be much worse. I was used to getting in trouble with foster families, and most of the time I didn't care. But this time was different. It wasn't like I wanted to hurt the McCrarys. I just didn't want anyone hurting Big Momma.

Mrs. McCrary was sitting on the living room couch, her hands folded on her lap like she was in after-school detention, which was backward because if anyone was going to wind up in *lifetime* detention, it was me. Big L had the *Snooze* spread open on the coffee table in front of him. Nothing was cut out of it. Sickmub didn't look up at me. Even the dog had me in the doghouse. Striker was sitting in the armchair. He held up the cut-up version of the newspaper and looked through it like it was a window to the outside and I was some really nasty weather.

"Did you really think you'd get away with this?" Big L asked. "Did you really think we wouldn't notice big holes cut out of the paper?"

I never know what to say when adults ask questions like that. What do they expect me to say? *No, I didn't think I'd get away with it.* Because then they'd ask, *So why on earth did you do it?* But if I say, *Sure, I expected to get away with it,* then, they'd say, *Do you think we're idiots?*

And how am I supposed to answer *that* question?

"Our own dog," Big L continued. "You got Babe tangled up in this. Babe on the front page!"

The McCrarys looked pretty hot, but at least they weren't the smacking type. I waited for them to start yelling and hollering. I would know how to handle that. I would sit there looking blank or sorry and wait for them to run out of scream—or steam—and that would be that. Then, I'd go to my room and start packing because I knew the social worker would be coming to pick me up soon.

Or maybe this time, Ike and I would climb out the window and run away. And then the McCrarys would have to call the Forest Glen police, and they'd hunt me down like I'm a cold-blooded killer, instead of just a kid who's getting kicked out of a foster home for defending the life of a living thing. It would take weeks for them to find me, and when they did, the story of my capture would appear in the *Snooze* crime blotter and everyone would be talking about me. Nobody in their right mind would ever want a foster kid who was an item in the crime blotter.

But that's not what happened. There was no yelling and hollering. It was worse than that. Much worse.

"Have a seat," Mrs. McCrary said. She motioned to the other armchair. "We need to have a big talk."

Not a big talk! I don't have anything against talking. I love to talk. But that's not what Mrs. McCrary meant. She meant *they* were going to talk and I was going to listen. I had to listen and not crack sunflower seeds, and I had to have the right look in my eyes and say the exact right thing at the exact right time. Big talks with adults are what banana slugs must feel when a really mean kid sprinkles salt on them. They dry out, twisting and shriveling into a painful death.

Big L looked me hard in the eyes. I twisted.

"Young lady, do you understand how much embarrassment you've caused us?"

Here we go again. If I said no, then Big L would want to know, *How can you NOT understand?*

If I said yes, he'd ask, *So why did you do it, then? Don't you appreciate that we took you in under our roof?* Then I'd have to answer *those* questions.

I shriveled.

Mrs. McCrary tried, "Termite, what you did was wrong. You agree with that much, don't you?"

I wiggled. I shrugged. Big L was starting to look furious. "At least she can apologize," he said to Mrs. McCrary. Then to me, "Do you want to apologize?"

If I said no, they'd ask, *Who do you think you are that you can't even offer an apology?* If I caved in and said I was sorry, they'd say, *We can tell you really don't mean it.*

At least that would be the truth. I wasn't sorry.

This is the reason that big talks make my head spin. I get crazy trying to figure out what I should say. Crazy and tired. I yawned. I yawned again.

"So rude." Mrs. McCrary sighed in disappointment.

Big L threw up his hands and said, "Grounded."

I almost said "yippee," because house arrest was way better than two minutes more of big talk. "How long?" I asked.

"Every day after school and all weekend for a start. Long enough for you to sit and think about what you've done."

Mrs. McCrary turned to Striker. "You've been pretty quiet there, son. Do you want to say anything?"

He shook his head. Nothing. He had nothing to say. But I had something I wanted to say to him. I was already grounded, so why not? "Striker, you care about that tree too. I know you do!"

He started to say something back, but his father beat him to it. "Striker cares about his family. He's almost a man, and a man has to make choices. In this case, he's making the right one."

I stood right in Striker's line of vision. "But what about you-know-what? Living you-know-where? How's that going to happen?"

He stood and took Sickmub by the collar. "You're an outsider, Termite. An outsider can't really understand. Let it go. My dad's right. I have to stick with my family."

twenty-seven

I can pat my head and rub my belly. I can do homework while watching TV and eating sunflower seeds. But I can't sit still and think at the same time. One social worker said that Motion is my middle name. It's not. My middle name is Ellen. But the point is that I need to pace while I do my thinking. I covered my entire bedroom, every inch of it.

Sometimes my thinking went like this: *Termite, you can't take on the whole town yourself.*

Sometimes my thinking sounded like a social worker: *Apologize like you mean it. You're in a good foster home. Do what you have to do to stay here.*

Sometimes my thinking sounded like Big L, and I had to admit that he made sense: *The family has been logging here for generations. Remember that eagle? Shouldn't members of this family be able to stay on their land and earn a living?*

But then my thinking sounded like something else. It was more of a feeling than an actual thought with words. I remembered what Mr. Cator had shown me in the nature book earlier that day. He had opened to a page with a drawing of a termite. I studied it hard. It was small and pale like me. The book said that the termite is very social, has a huge appetite, and can really wreck buildings and furniture. True, true, true. About the bug and me. To most people, the termite is just a great big nuisance.

Then Mr. Cator said that when termites are living in the woods, it's a whole other story. The termite can't be called destructive then. It's just doing its job, the job that nature intended, and nature doesn't make mistakes. In the wilderness, away from houses and buildings, where the termite is supposed to be, it only breaks down trees that have already fallen. Mr. Cator really emphasized that. "The termite has gotten a bad reputation. People think it's destructive, but it has an extremely beneficial role. It converts dead trees into matter that helps other trees and plants live. The forest really depends on the termite."

I kicked at a pile of dirty laundry on my bedroom floor. Maybe I was kicking at all the voices that were telling me that whatever happened to the forest was none of my business. Maybe I was kicking at the other fosters, at the

McCrarys, at Striker, for trying to hold me back from doing what I knew I had to do.

I wasn't an outsider anymore. There was a place I belonged. I had been to the inside of Big Momma, way up on her branches, surrounded by her smell. I had been to the inside of the tree, and now the tree was inside of me.

I made a decision.

The entire forest, from the biggest redwood to the banana slug, was depending on the help of the small but Mighty Termite.

◆

I started writing the official chronicle of what happened next, which I titled THE ADVENTURES OF THE MIGHTY TERMITE.

The Mighty Termite remembered how Striker—once her friend, now her enemy—said that she'd have no trouble surviving in the woods. "Piece of cake," he said. And that reminded her that there was cake left over from dinner, so the Mighty Termite with the mighty appetite tiptoed down the stairs and wrapped a slab of double-chocolate in plastic wrap and shoved it into her pocket.

Who knew how long it would take to complete her dangerous solo mission? She needed more supplies, so she found a basket and put together her famous

Basket o'Crap, which is what she does whenever she takes off from a foster home. She got the idea from the gift baskets that people give each other for Christmas. Only instead of expensive smelly cheese and crackers, the Mighty Termite raided the pantry and put together all her personal food favorites— double-cream-filled cookies, a jar of pickles, ranch-flavored corn chips, a six-pack of cola, a banana, sunflower seeds, of course, and a jar of marshmallow fluff. She also packed a tin of anchovies because Paul Bunyan types recommend always packing a disgusting food you don't like, so you don't snack on it. Then, if you really run out of food and you're ready to die of starvation, the disgusting food will still be there. How genius is that?

The Mighty Termite also put her trusted companion, the former general Ike Eisenhower, into the basket. This doesn't mean she thought Ike was crap. Not for a minute! The Mighty Termite needed a free hand for carrying her light source (flashlight).

Her final step was to pull her official M² Banana Slug sweatshirt over her head and jam some things into the pockets and into her backpack. Matches, some rope, masking tape, plastic garbage bags— because the motto of the Mighty Termite is "Don't litter! Pack your trash."

After writing so much, my brain was fried, so I switched to drawing. Since I'm a bad artist, it was cartoon drawing. Cartoon hands can look like this:

and nobody complains, "Those don't look like real hands!"

The next part of the story went like this:

It took a lot of work to draw a pitch-black sky. By then my hand was falling off and the pen was almost out of ink, so I have to tell the next part of the story without any pictures. I have to tell it just as it happened.

twenty-eight

There was the Big Momma tree in the dark, creeeeepy with five *E*s, even to someone who's run from foster homes in the middle of the night. More candles, an American flag, and a sign: RESPECT YOUR ELDERS. SAVE THE MOTHER OF THE FOREST. The printing was even worse than mine, like someone was trying to disguise their handwriting.

"Who's here?" I asked.

Silence. The fog had rolled in so thick I could run my hands through it and separate it into swirls and circles. Uh-oh. Ghost time. I dumped my stuff on the ground and shined the light to my left and my right, spinning around suddenly like police on TV do when they have a criminal cornered.

Maybe flattery would work. Everyone, even a psycho-killer-voodooist forest creature, likes to hear they've done a good job.

"Whoever you are, you really outdid yourself. The American flag, nice touch."

More silence, and something about that quiet really got to me this time. It stopped being creepy; it was rude. I was tired of being ignored. I had been patient, patient enough. It wasn't fair. There were only two of us in the whole world who were determined to protect Big Momma, two of us who were willing to go against the entire town. Two people like that should at least talk to each other. "A person can take only so much of the silent treatment," I said. "Show yourself to the Mighty Termite!"

Did someone just snort? Or was it the wind?

"Don't show yourself then! See if the Mighty Termite cares. I have business to take care of."

That showed him. Or her. Or it.

After that, it was on to the reason I was here in the middle of the night, freezing my bottom off. The forest was depending on me. I was supposed to be doing something. Only I wasn't sure exactly what. I could protest. That's what forest savers do. But how exactly do you do that? Whatever Heartsong did didn't look all that hard. I lit some of the candles, sat cross-legged in front of Big Momma, and chanted "oooooooo, Maaaaaaaaaa."

Correction. It was hard. Impossible. A lot of social workers have suggested that a ball of energy like me should try meditating. It's supposed to make me calm by erasing my thoughts. But man-oh-man, it backfired. By the time I chanted "ooooooo, Maaaaaa" four times, my head felt like there was a Ping-Pong ball bouncing around in there. I was so antsy that I wanted to scream. So I did scream. A couple of birds took off. The truth is, I don't *want* to calm my thoughts. I like them. All of them. I like the way they hop around and bump into each other, the way they snap and pop.

I put a leaf into the fire of one of the candles. It made a sound. It exploded. Like that! That's the way I like my thoughts to feel.

A new thought rushed in, and it gave me a warm, familiar feeling. I imagined how everyone I knew in Forest Glen was tucked into bed and would soon be waking up, brushing their teeth, getting dressed, and sitting down to a logger's breakfast. Mrs. McCrary as always in her bathrobe flipping pancakes, pouring on the syrup. Mmmmm. Bread with a big slab of jam.

Next thoughts: What am I doing out here? Should I sneak back into the house before anyone notices I'm missing?

Yes! No! Yes! No!

That built up an appetite. I dug into the Basket o' Crap and ate a banana and a pickle and washed them down with soda. That took five minutes.

I lit some more candles. That took forty-five seconds.

I tried the meditating thing again. I let my eyes roll to

the top of my head and jiggle like marbles under my eye-lids. Three minutes.

I messed with the wax in the candles. Two minutes.

I messed with the wax in my ears. Two minutes.

I threw Douglas fir cones at a tree and counted how many times I hit the target. Fifteen out of twenty. Five minutes.

Would the McCrarys miss me when they noticed I was gone? Ten seconds.

I peed in the woods. Four minutes. It would have only taken three minutes, but I walked pretty far to make sure that the psycho-killer-voodooist didn't get a free show.

I let loose with a great big noisy yawn, the kind that goes on for about a minute. I yawned again. Maybe it was too late at night to save the forest. I could get started for real in the morning.

There weren't too many spots on the ground that weren't bumpy or full of prickly things. I settled on a place not far from Big Momma. I kicked aside the biggest cones and moved a banana slug so he wouldn't get suffocated. From my backpack, I took out the garbage bags and spread them like a tarp. The ferns and moss below gave it a soft base. I switched off the flashlight.

Not bad. Not bad at all. I wasn't scared. Lots of people have survived a night alone in the woods.

Wind whistled through the trees.

Dogs barked from way off in the distance.

A branch hit the ground. *Bam!*

Drip-drip-drip. What was that?

I swear I heard the giant puffball mushrooms growing and slurping up food from deep in the soil. I did!

Some animals started making weird noises that sounded like someone giggling and gargling at the same time. Coyotes. That was the worst. Okay, maybe I was scared. Honeysuckle was always saying that if you say positive things out loud, they have a better chance of making you feel better. I stood up and announced, "I'm the Mighty Termite! I'm not scared."

It didn't help at all.

I thought of one other thing to say. I spoke directly into the darkness. "Hey, you out there. It's okay with me if you want to spend the rest of the night here too. I don't mind. Only, me right here, you over there. *Way* over there. It'll be like a sleepover. Sort of. Except without the pizza."

That helped a little. Only now I was freezing. I was sure my chattering teeth would shatter my head. I got back on top of the garbage bags, curled myself into a tight ball and pulled my sweatshirt hood tight over my ears.

I really could have used Sickmub and his warm fur right then. I also thought of Mrs. McCrary, how one night she had tried to tuck me in. I was too old for that! But still, almost every night she came into my room.

"Good night, you," she would say and then rumple my uncombed hair until I pushed her hand away.

◆

I must have fallen asleep. I know this because something woke me. I call it God light. It's the kind of early morning light that slants through the clouds and trees and makes you think that music will start playing and someone will come sliding down the beam straight from heaven.

There was another miracle that morning. I had gone to sleep with nothing covering me and woke with a blue blanket wrapped tight. I should have been spooked, but I was just warm and grateful. I sat up, rubbed the sleep from my eyes, and took in the new day.

At first, it seemed exactly like the enchanted forest where all the animals are waiting on Snow White. Any minute I expected birds to swoop down and tie my hair back with a bow. Maybe some rabbits would powder my face with their cottontails. But that was before reality sunk in. My pal the Steller's jay squawked and made a big poop. During the night, I must have rolled off the garbage bags because when I touched my cheek, there was the perfect impression of a redwood cone. The forest had also littered all over me, twigs, needles, dust, bark, and seeds. My hands were numb, white at the fingertips. Plus, I was starved. Food now! There was still a pickle left. I ate it, followed by two big spoonfuls of Marshmallow Fluff. The anchovies could wait.

Now what was I supposed to do? Protect the forest, of course, but at the moment, there was no one to protect it from. *Hum-hum-hum,* I hummed. I ate some more Fluff.

There sure are a lot of hours to fill up in a day. The sun wasn't even all the way up yet and I was already getting bored. I needed a boredom buster. WWMCD?

What **W**ould **M**r. **C**ator **D**o?

He would walk around picking up interesting rock specimens. So that's what I did. He would watch a daddy longlegs creep along a redwood stump until it trapped and ate a pill bug. After that, he would rush over and double-check that the lid to Ike Eisenhower's mayonnaise jar was extra tight. Maybe Mr. Cator wouldn't do that, but I sure did.

Then he would watch some baby dragonflies and not really believe what he saw. They shoot water out their butts, which moves them forward like jets. He would watch this ten times to make sure that he really saw this right because no one was going to believe it.

Mr. Cator would probably set up a science fair project right on the spot and answer the question, *How do momma slugs make sure that baby slugs don't get lost or squished?* The conclusion turned out *not* to be an answer

I wanted to know. The momma slugs don't do a thing! I found a mess of eggs tucked beside a log, and right while I was watching, the babies hatched. But was there a mother to greet them? No! Was there a mother to show them the best things to eat or how to hide from enemies? Double no!

This whole situation got me angry. I was stewing. I wanted to find that banana slug mother and get right in her face. *How can you abandon your kids that way? Who's going to take care of them?* The banana slug world wasn't any better than the human world. Only the strongest, the smartest, the luckiest slugs were going to survive.

But then, Striker's words came back to remind me: *There are no mistakes of nature.* Every banana slug mother takes off, not just a few like in the human world. So, there's probably a good reason for why the kids are left on their own. The banana slug kids, I mean, not the human ones. There's no real good reason for that.

"Good luck, baby banana slugs," I said.

By this time, the God light had disappeared. The fog was back in, and everything was gray. My blanket had become useless against the *drip-drip-drip.* So I came up with another idea. I ripped a hole in one of the large garbage bags and put my head through it. A rain cape. For a hat, I used a smaller garbage bag.

Now what? I decided to try meditating again. Maybe if I had a better attitude about it. I heard that if you really work at it, you can leave your own body. I wouldn't mind my foot falling asleep if it meant I would mysteriously lift a hundred feet off the ground into a dimension that only a select few of the living ever get to experience.

I sat by the tree and closed my eyes.

"Ooooooooo, Maaaaaaaaaaaaaaaa." Think light thoughts. *Light, light, light.* It was working! I was close—this close!—to leaving my body. No wonder I didn't hear the *crunch-crunch* of footsteps coming into the clearing.

"What is it?" a voice said. That snapped me out of my trance. My eyes opened.

Four figures stood at the edge of the trail. I squinted to get a better look, but the fog erased any details. One of them said, "I could be wrong here. But I think it's a girl. In a garbage bag."

"Dang! Scared the bejesus out of me."

"One of those *oooooo maaaa* protesters."

"Ah, she's just a bitty thing. Shouldn't give us any problem."

Two of the voices sounded familiar. One belonged to William J. Reener, Diane's dad and lumber company vice president. The other voice said, "You fellas get started. Guess I should be the one to have a big talk with the young lady here."

As the figure came closer, something in the woods behind me moved quickly and softly. Maybe it was an animal. But I didn't think so. This moved in a different way, like something that knows these woods even better than a deer does.

twenty-nine

"Young lady, you had us all worried. I would have had the police out looking for you if Striker hadn't convinced me that you're a resourceful little thing. Young lady—"

"Don't call me that!" I said.

"Call you what?"

"Young lady! That's all you ever call me. I'm a foster kid, but I got a name. Do you even know my name?"

"That's not the issue here."

"When someone has things in common with you, like you said, when someone's seen you depressed in your bathrobe, you should know their name. If you want to talk to me, call me Termite."

"Okay, Termite."

"The Mighty Termite."

Big L made a sound that made his lips vibrate. "The *Mighty* Termite. Happy now? We have work to do here. You made your point, so head back home. If you hurry, you still have time to catch the school bus."

I pulled off the garbage bag from my head. "Nope."

"Nope?"

"I made a promise."

"To who?"

"To Big Momma." I patted the bark behind me.

I figured that Big L was going to turn red and start yelling, but he did the opposite. His face went soft, like the time he took Striker and me to see the eagle. He eased himself onto the ground next to me and leaned his back against the tree.

"Listen, Termite. Mighty Termite. I'm not one of the bad guys like those tree-huggers make us out to be. None of us are. If anyone loves this forest, it's those of us who have lived here all our lives."

"That's why you can't let this happen. You know how much Striker loves this tree. You can't kill it for no reason."

"That's right. I wouldn't destroy something for no reason."

I thought, *He agrees! My one-termite protest has saved the day!* I was so excited. I jumped up and did the tail-feather-shaking, hula-karate, happy chicken, and stomp-out-a-fire dances. The men watched for a second, then went back to what they were doing, which was walking quietly around the forest. Each one had a clipboard that they kept checking. Every now and then, they stopped in front of a tree and tied a ribbon around it. Soon, the forest was covered with pink bows, like it was being decorated for a princess theme party.

I was a little out of breath. "So, what are the pink bows for?"

Big L didn't say anything. I ran his words through my head again. *I wouldn't destroy something for no reason.*

"Oh!" I said. Then "Oh!" again. "You think you have a reason!"

He blew out the candles, stood, and used the toe of his big boot to kick aside the pile of feathers, cones, and bones. "If I didn't think it was absolutely necessary." The stack of stones tumbled down. "Go home now."

I didn't budge. Big L took his time tying the biggest, pinkest ribbon around Big Momma's belly. "I am home," I said.

Then I budged. Fast!

◇

In a small town like Forest Glen, you didn't need to watch TV or listen to the radio. News traveled on its own. Word of what I was up to got out fast. Honeysuckle told me later that everyone was talking about it.

"She's up the tree."

"Who's up the tree?"

"That Termite girl!"

"Just zipped right up there, like she really was half-termite."

"Says she won't come down until she's sure that nobody touches Big Momma."

News traveled fast, but a lot of it traveled wrong. There were all kinds of weird rumors about me. First Honeysuckle heard that loggers had drugged me with too much Ritalin and were holding me hostage. Then she heard that I was at the very top of the tree and threatening to jump! Then she heard that I had already fallen out and my brains were splattered all over the ground. Then people were saying that I had gone native, turned into a full-blown forest creature, and was eating banana slugs.

Here's the news that's the truth. Before Big L could stop me, I hurried around to the side of Big Momma and scooted up the limb of the Douglas fir, up the rope and onto the first branch. I could have stopped there, but my climbing brain took over and I wrapped my arms and legs back around the rope. As I passed each new branch, I made my commitment firmer. *I won't abandon the tree. I won't stop until I sit at the very heart of Big Momma.* At the fifth branch, the rope ended in a big knot. Using momentum, I swung myself closer to the limb and trapped it in my legs. When I knew I could make it safely, I let go of the rope and transferred my weight. Sitting on the branch, I hung my legs over the side and took a minute to catch my breath. I remembered that I still had a piece of cake in my pocket. By this point, it was smooshed and gooey, but licking that chocolate off my fingers, I don't think I ever tasted anything that good in my whole life.

From a branch above me, a banana slug on a slime string dropped in front of my eyes. That would have been enough to send most kids hurling backward out of the tree. But I recognized this particular slug. "Maxine?" I asked. The slug didn't move. "Maxine!"

From below, I could hear voices. My name was being yelled—"Termite!"—and lots of words that I couldn't make out clearly. Then I heard a loud electronic screech, followed by my name again—**TERMITE!**—coming from something that sounded like a karaoke machine.

Now what? What do I do? I couldn't just sit there all day. I was there to make a point. I needed to get them to understand what the tree meant to me, to all of us. I stood, held on to the overhead branch for support, and slowly inched my way out from the center of the tree. The limb under my feet got thinner, and it sagged a little under my weight. Above me, something cracked.

"Widow-maker," someone yelled. A branch flew past. The karaoke voice again: **"You up there! Stop! Don't do anything foolish! And don't look down!"**

I looked down. Isn't that what people do when some-one shouts "don't look down"? The voice came from a policeman speaking into a bullhorn. That surprised me. I didn't expect a policeman. I also didn't expect to see so many people so soon. There were a lot of them, even more than the time in my ninth foster home, when a kid dared me to climb to the top of an old radio transmis-sion tower and I got halfway up.

It seemed like everyone in town was down there now. Foster parents and teachers, the librarian, waitresses from Edna's Tree Hut. Mr. Cator in his shorts. From this height, even the Hoppers looked small, like toy boys from a doll-house. A group of foster kids stood together, looking up at me, worried. I could see Mr. and Mrs. McCrary talk-ing to my social worker.

Striker was down there too, shoulders hunched, hands in his back pockets, kicking at dirt. I wanted him to look up, to have our eyes lock. If he did, what would I yell down to him? *Come on! Help! I don't think I can do this alone. It's just me, one kid.*

No! I wouldn't say that. Not to a traitor, not to some-one who turned his back on Big Momma. I could do this by myself. I would!

"Hey, Sickmub!" I yelled. The dog started barking and wagging his tail, looking everywhere for me, up, left, behind a rock, all crazy happy to hear my voice. That felt good. What didn't feel good was when the Hopper cousins started the chant, "Whack 'em! Stack 'em! Rack 'em! Pack 'em!" Someone shouted, "Terminate the Termite." Even some adults joined in. "Start the logging! Drag her down!"

The voice on the bullhorn returned. **"Termite! The next voice you hear will be that of your social worker."**

The next voice: **"Listen to reason. This will accomplish nothing."**

"I made a promise!" I yelled.

"What? What are you saying?"

"A promise!"

"A kiss? You want a kiss? Who do you want to kiss?"

"Termite, this is Mrs. McCrary. Come down. No one will send you to another foster home. I promise."

"This is William J. Reener, vice president of the North Coast Lumber Company. You are on private property. This is costing our company time and money. Enough polite talk."

Mr. Reener's eyes scanned the crowd and then landed on someone. He continued talking through the bullhorn. **"You, McCrary. Yeah, you. Get her down."**

The chanting picked up. "Get her down! Get her down!"

Big L stepped away from his wife and Striker. He took two steps forward, looked back at them. He didn't look happy about it, but he headed my way.

thirty

First came Josh.

I didn't expect him to be first because a kid who spends most of his day in a box usually shrivels and turns to dust when anyone even looks at him. So, surprise of surprises, Josh was the first to stick out his neck.

Actually, it was more than his neck. He stretched out his whole body on the fallen limb of the Douglas fir. Genius! Wherever Big L tried to put his foot on the branch, Josh scooted forward or backward so that his face was right there. It was a brave move. One of Big L's boots must have weighed twenty pounds, and the bottom was probably thick with dirt and slug slime and stinging nettle juice, and Josh would have gotten a mouthful of it.

Big L finally gave up, but only after Mr. Cator whispered something to him that made Big L shrug. Mr. Cator slapped him on the back in the friendly man-to-man way. Then Big L disappeared from view for a while. When I spotted him again, he was at a far corner of the clearing, squatting by a pile of climbing equipment.

Second came Honeysuckle. Third came Lupe, and Charlie was fourth.

They spaced themselves around the base of the tree. They tried to hold hands, but their fingers didn't come anywhere near reaching. Someone else rushed out of the crowd.

"Connie! Don't!" her foster father yelled.

Two more foster kids ran out with her, and together they formed a perfect ring. Then pretty much every foster kid in Forest Glen stepped forward and sat down, forming a bigger circle outside of the first ring. I pumped my fist in the air and shouted, "Way to go! Power Rings of eccentric circles!"

"*Con*centric!" Honeysuckle yelled back.

"Traitors!" Portapotty #1 shouted.

"Outsiders!" #2 yelled. "Go back where you belong."

Others joined in.

"You don't fit in Forest Glen."

"You don't fit anywhere!"

"No one wants you here!"

"Let's bust up those circles!"

From somewhere in the crowd, someone threw a

cone. Redwood cones might be small, but hurled at thirty miles an hour, they sting. It hit Charlie behind the ear, hard enough to make him yell. In the commotion, someone else sneaked up and dropped a banana slug down the back of Lupe's shirt. Big L tried to step through the Power Rings, but the foster kid power proved too much for him.

Mr. Reener was on the bullhorn again. **"Attention! One, two, three, four. Can you all hear me? How about you up there? I have been informed by both the chief of police and the Department of Children's Services that all of you are trespassers. Not only are you breaking the law, but you are runaways from your foster homes and therefore can be—"**

A voice came from out of the crowd. "Mr. Reener! I have something to say."

Striker! What could he possibly want to say? The same thing as everyone else.

"Okay, Striker. Step right up here!" Mr. Reener handed over the bullhorn and Striker put it to his mouth. I listened carefully.

"You all know me, right?"

The Portapotties did high-fives. Diane and her girl-friends said, "Goooo, Striker."

"You know that I was born right here. That I'm the son of a logger and the grandson of a logger."

"One of us," someone said.

"I'm not an outsider. I'm not a foster kid."

"You show 'em, Striker."

So that's what he did. Exactly what he did.

"Come here, Babe." The dog followed him. When they got to the very edge of the Power Rings, the fosters linked arms even more tightly. Striker waited, like he expected Honeysuckle and the others to give up just because he was standing there. He tilted back his head and cupped his hands to his mouth. "Termite, tell them to let me through."

"Are you kidding? No way!" I yelled back down.

"I mean it, Termite."

"Why should I?"

Striker didn't answer.

"Give me one good reason."

"Because," he began. "Because . . . you just have to trust me on this one. You have to trust somebody."

Our eyes met and, even from way up high—*click*—I saw things in them that I thought I recognized. I *hoped* I recognized. Anger and fear and sadness and determination. I was the only one who could see Striker's eyes right then, and I was looking at someone about to do the hardest thing he'd ever done in his life. He needed my help, and I needed his.

Honeysuckle was waiting for me to tell her what to do next. Hesitant, still not sure, I raised my hand, the thumb pointing up in the air. She dropped the hand next to hers. Others followed her lead, and soon there was a clear pathway to the base of the tree. For a moment, Striker looked confused, like he had forgotten why he was there and how he had gotten there and if he even wanted to be there. But I supposed he was just gathering strength.

He walked to the base of the tree and got down on one knee. He arranged a pile of cones and placed a bird feather into the center of it. "Anyone have a match?" he yelled. He didn't have to wait. I knew what he was doing then. I guess I'd known for a long time. I dropped a pack of matches, which he caught without even looking up. First, he lit the blue candle, then the yellow one, and then the red.

He lit them, as he had lit them so many times before.

"Striker?" someone asked from the crowd.

"Babe! Sit!" he ordered, then scratched the dog under the neck. "Stay here and guard."

On the other side of the tree, no one had to tell Josh what to do. Quickly, he moved aside. Striker kicked off his shoes and scrambled up the slippery fallen log to the rope. No hands! Bare feet! In no time, he was climbing, past the first branch and the second.

Then, there was Striker in his flannel shirt, dots of sweat at his temples, scratches on his face, sitting next to me on the branch.

"No shoes?" I asked him.

"Can't climb as well with them on. Too much separation between me and the tree."

"Here," I said and handed him the last of the chocolate cake.

That was our whole conversation for a while. I had a lot on my mind. We both did. But at the same time, what was there to say?

I took my bag of sunflower seeds out of my pocket. We cracked and spit, watching the shells drop into the branches below. Striker and me, two kids from different worlds, standing up—no, sitting down—for something much bigger than either one of us.

Wasn't that enough for right then? Didn't that say it all?

thirty-one

A clap of thunder? Compared to the sound I heard in the forest, that would be just a whisper.

A rock concert? A jet going faster than the speed of light? That's only quiet humming.

Man-oh-man, I never heard a sound like the sound of a tree falling. *Sound* doesn't even begin to describe it. Neither do any of these words: *Loud. Thump. Thud. Bang. Clobber. Hit. Whack.* That's because words are just things you hear with your ears.

That afternoon, when the first tree went down, it was like a slap across your face. A slap across your face when you didn't do anything wrong. A slap across your face when you didn't do anything wrong and there's nobody to complain to and the person who slapped you has curled-up lips that say "that was for your own good."

That kind of sound. A slap across your face that you feel down in your liver and kidneys. You can't feel anything deeper than that. That's the sound a redwood tree makes when it hits the forest floor.

◇

Here's a science-teacher question if there ever was one: If a tree falls in the forest, and no one's around to hear it, does it make a sound?

I had never understood why kids in class get all worked up over that one. One genius kid waves his arms in the air, saying, "Yes! Yes! There's a sound!" and blah-blahing about the wave motions and air disturbance. Then another kid gets smug and makes a show-offy snort and says, "I beg to differ." Then she starts talking about ear-drums and vibrating ear bones and the whole commotion makes me say, "It's some dumb old tree in a forest! Why get all worked up about that?" Once I got sent into the hallway to calm down and to think about respecting the opinions of my fellow students.

But now I understood. I needed to know the answer. "What do you think?" I asked Striker after that first tree went down.

He explained the scientific argument about eardrums and bones and how sound waves need something to vibrate against to really be considered sound. He's a good teacher.

I almost understood it, but I didn't buy it. Neither did Striker.

From across the clearing, we could hear chainsaws starting up again. When another tree went down, Striker waited for the air to stop vibrating. He said, "Even if no one's around, not even a banana slug, a tree falling makes a sound the whole world can hear."

I let this sink in, we both did. Then he asked, "What are we waiting for?"

I dared him, "Beat you to the top!"

thirty-two

I kicked off my shoes, watched them drop. They bounced off branches, skipped in different directions before disappearing. I waited but I didn't hear them hit bottom. Just think. My smelly old shoes trapped in Big Momma forever. I liked that idea. Parent chickadees could take them over for a nest, teaching their babies to use the tongues as runways for flying lessons.

Time to climb.

I twisted around so that I was facing the trunk and had something firm to hold on to as I stood. I arched both feet around the branch for an extra tight grip. Striker was right about how it felt good to feel the tree directly, like there was no difference at all between skin and bark. Only, if the bark had been human, it would have needed some skin lotion or hair conditioner because it was rough and shaggy. That's okay for a red-wood, though. Some things depend on a thick skin to survive.

"You coming?" he shouted. He was only a branch above me, but all I could see of him was from the ankles down.

"Of course I'm coming! What do you think?"

"You're not scared, are you?"

"I wish there was a rope."

"You can do it, Termite. Look up. The branches are fairly evenly spaced, like it's a ladder."

Here's where you're probably thinking that it must have been a snap to follow Striker up the tree. Maybe you think, *All she had to do was follow in his footsteps.* But that's not the way climbing works. A certain path may be right for one person, but that doesn't mean it works for everyone. Skinny, speedy termite muscles can't do the same things as bigger, bulkier logger-kid muscles. You can't count on the person above to find the best path for you. That's a fact of life, whether you're climbing a tree or trying any other new hard thing.

Repeat this ten times: *You have to find your own way up.*

If you run out of breath, nobody can breathe for you. I was on my own. It was just me and my own arms and legs and stomach muscles. The only thing that the person who went first can do is what Striker did for me. He kept encouraging. "Piece of cake, Termite. You're doing great. Keep going."

I climbed like a maaaniac with four *A*s. One branch, then another. This was the highest I'd ever been in my life, higher than any roof of any foster home, higher even than the transmission tower. It was as if all my other climbing had been preparing me for this. I needed to get to the very top, needed to know what the air smelled like up there, how far I could see, if I could see to the edge of world.

For every branch I reached, Striker must have scaled two or three. I was only halfway up when I heard shouts and a voice from the bullhorn.

"Attention! You! Striker! The North Coast Lumber Company will not prosecute if you come down now peacefully."

More *eek*ing and *aah*ing and *ooh*ing. What was Striker doing? Was he saying something back? I needed to know.

I reached overhead, stretched high enough on tiptoes to grab on to the low-hanging branch above me. Slowly, I inched out from the center of the tree. My left foot slipped on something. I caught myself by jamming my foot into the nearest nook. That brilliant move kept me from sliding off, but it also made something snap. In my foot. A toe. Left foot, the toe next to the pinkie.

I knew it was broken because suddenly my heart was in my foot—*pump-thump-pump*—and it hurt. But I reminded myself that you don't die from a broken toe. It just turns the shape of a cheese twist, a purple one.

I continued inching away from the trunk until the branch wasn't much thicker than my bony leg. Still, it was worth the trip, the broken toe and everything. I craned my neck and saw what everyone down below was *aah*ing about.

At almost the very top stood Striker, his legs spread apart, nothing but foggy sky above. A spotlight arced across the tree, settled on him, held him in the light. Striker's arms stretched open in a way that made him look less like a boy and more like another limb sprouting out of Big Momma. He looked comfortable up there, in the same way that Big L's old eagle had looked comfortable. At home. Like they'd been there forever, and they would always be there. Both of them. The eagle in his tree and the boy in *his* tree.

Alone, but not lonely.

I heard another snap.

This time it wasn't a toe. It was wood.

I reached out for something to grab. There was nothing.

Nothing except for a rush of air whistling in my ears, the smack of branches, and the sight of the forest floor rushing up to meet me.

◇

They said I was lucky. They said I was very, very, *very* lucky. Maybe the luckiest kid in the world.

Man-oh-man, I wouldn't call it lucky to be crashed on the ground with redwood twigs up your nose and feeling like an elephant was taking a nap on your chest. I don't really don't know what it feels like to have an elephant napping on my chest. That's just one of those figures of speech, but it couldn't have been much worse than what I felt.

I guess there are all degrees of luckiness. I was lucky that I didn't fall out of a tree into a convention of unicorns. I was the kind of lucky that when you're falling from a tree, an instinct tells you to reach out and grab ahold of something—anything!—so that it stops your fall a little, just enough so that Big Momma catches you in a branchy cradle for a few seconds.

Those seconds mean everything. They slow you down enough so that it isn't like you fell off a ten-story tree, but more like a two-story tree.

Instead of being crashed on the forest floor with my brains smashed up for slug food, I was on the forest floor with my left leg in some funny position, like it wasn't even attached to my body.

Not funny like in ha-ha-ha-ha. Funny like in uh-oh.

If you want to call that lucky, go ahead.

I opened my eyes. All the people of Forest Glen—the teachers and loggers and TV newspeople, Diane Reener, the Portapotties, the cafeteria lunch lady, a fireman, Honeysuckle, Mr. Reener—were bent over me saying things like "do you need an aspirin?"

"Do you need water?"

"Can you breathe?"

"Give her air!"

"Cover her up!"

"Move her here!"

"No! Don't move her at all."

"I'm so sorry, Termite."

"We're all sorry."

More faces moved in, three of them. The features were blurry. I blinked once, twice. One face came into focus—Striker with a big cut on his cheek. Then the other faces. Mr. McCrary pressing his hands against his lips. Mrs. McCrary, her face more pale than I'd ever seen it.

Striker asked, "Termite, are you okay? Are you?"

Did I look okay?

I didn't get a chance to say that because the elephant that really wasn't there shifted its weight and the faces, the forest, everything disappeared.

thirty-three

If I had a scrapbook—which I don't because I change houses too much and I would probably lose it—but if I did have a scrapbook, I'd have a special place for the article that appeared the next day in the *Snooze.*

I didn't get to read the article that day or even the next. I was in the hospital, drifting in and out of sleep, feeling pains in parts of my body that I didn't even know existed.

◇

Honeysuckle was one of the first visitors I had in the hospital. She sat in the chair next to my really cool hospital bed that I could move up and down with the push of a button.

"If you stop fooling around with that bed for a second, I'll read you the article," she said.

LOGGERS SPARE BIG MOMMA TREE
Two Protesters—One at Top and One at Bottom—Get Promise from North Coast Lumber Company

A heroic band of youngsters risked their lives and refused to leave until North Coast Lumber met some of their demands. . . . No one will be prosecuted and sent to juvenile hall. And no one will harm Big Momma.

On the front page, there were lots of pictures, a great one of me passed out with drool on the corner of my mouth and an even better one of Striker near the top of the tree. There was also a photo of Josh and Mr. Cator posing with banana slugs on their shoulders. In another picture, it looks like the photographer had climbed a nearby tree because the photo looked down on the Power Rings. You could make out everyone's face. Sickmub was standing guard. That dog's okay. He didn't budge all day, except to come over and lick my face after I fell.

I spent almost two weeks in the hospital and then the McCrarys took me back to their house. The first morning there, Striker woke me early. He helped with my crutches and together we made it into the woods.

When we got to the logged area, I didn't feel like much of a hero anymore. True, Big Momma was still there, but so many other trees had been cut down. They were still lying there, waiting to be dragged away and turned into someone's deck or furniture. Man-oh-man, it looked like the forest had been turned on its side.

It surprised me that Striker wasn't nearly as depressed about it as I was. "Trees grow back," he said. "It takes a long time, but it'll happen."

Leaning on both crutches, I bent over and picked up one of the pink bows. If I was a pink-bow kind of girl, I would have used it to make a ponytail. Instead, I looped it around my crutch. "At least they didn't clean-cut it."

"Clear-cut it," Striker said. He patted the bark of Big Momma. Then he looped his arm around my shoulders, and I didn't even think about shoving it off. "The company will replant. And as long as the mother tree is here, others will sprout from it."

◇

I figured it was only a matter of time before I started hearing, *Good-bye, foster kids! Good-bye, troublemakers!*

Some of the kids did leave Forest Glen. It was hard to tell the exact reason. That's the way life goes when you're a foster. Someone somewhere makes a decision and good-bye. Maybe some of the families didn't need the money anymore now that the logging was back. Maybe they had a troublemaker who drove them nuts. I've been *that* kid a couple of times. One of the fifth-grade fosters ran away just because she felt like it. Someone heard that she got all the way to Sacramento before the social workers caught up with her. I've been that kid too.

A few fosters left because they got better offers. Charlie's aunt and uncle in Los Angeles said that he could go live with them, and he jumped at the chance. He bragged that he was going to trade a thousand trees for a thousand cousins. One fifth-grader got picked up by his grandparents. Another was told that she could finally go home and live with her mother. That's a dream for a lot of foster kids. She seemed very happy and very nervous at the same time. "You'd have to know my mother to understand," she told us during lunch. Honeysuckle nodded because I think she has a mother just like that one.

Lupe was really surprised when her foster parents said that she could stay with them as long as she wanted, even though her foster father was working full-time at the mill. They didn't really need the money anymore, but they needed Lupe. They came right out and said that! "We need you. Our family wouldn't feel right without Lupe."

Lupe didn't know whether to believe them or not. Me either. Nobody had ever said anything like that to either of us before. Honeysuckle convinced her to stick around and see how things worked out. What did she have to lose?

Then there was Honeysuckle. Even when a foster irons her own jeans and never does anything wrong, it can still be good-bye. Honeysuckle's foster family could have decided that they wanted a boy foster kid or that they needed her bedroom for junk storage. She was really relieved when none of those things happened. She started loosening up and not worrying about everything so much all the time. Everyone—I mean everyone, including Diane Reener and the Hoppers—started coming to her for psychology advice about parents and best friends and their love lives. The new, improved Honeysuckle jumped to the top of Termite's popularity list and stayed in the number-two spot for an all-time record of seven months.

One more thing about Honeysuckle. Nobody knows this but me. Being part of the logging protest gave her a little taste of being bad and breaking rules. She liked it. She *really* liked it. After that, we did some very un-Honeysuckle-like things together, things that no one ever found out about. And I'm *not* about to tell them now.

◇

One Sunday afternoon a couple of months after we saved Big Momma and when my broken bones were getting back to normal, Connie's foster parents opened Edna's Tree Hut to the whole town. Free food for all. Honeysuckle's foster dad dressed up like a clown and handed out balloons. Music by the Hopper Family Bluegrass Band with the Portapotties playing washboards. A bunch of loggers grilled hot dogs with Mr. Cator in charge of buns. I had three with mustard. One more and I might have puked. No one knew what the big celebration was about.

After everyone was stuffed and the band was taking a break, Connie's foster father, Mr. Taylor, tapped a fork against a water glass. When everyone had their bottles and soda cans in the air, he toasted, "To Edna's great-granddaughter."

A lot of people didn't get it. I know I didn't get it at first. Mr. Taylor knew he was pulling off a good one because his mouth was trying to be serious but not doing a good job of it. The corners of his lips vibrated.

"Oh, don't leave them guessing!" Mrs. Taylor said. "To our new daughter. To our Connie. The adoption papers are all signed. Come here, honey. I think I'm gonna cry."

There were tears, all right, and not just from Mrs. Taylor. Then laughing, handshaking, and hugging. The music started again and everyone looked like they were going to bust a happiness vein in the middle of their foreheads.

I'm not big on kissing or crying or hugging for happiness. But I can really get into toasting. "To Connie!" I said and clicked soda cans with Honeysuckle, who said, "To Connie."

"To Big Momma tree!" Josh said, who clicked cans with me, Honeysuckle, Lupe, and Connie.

"To banana slugs everywhere!" *Click*.

"Ike Eisenhower!" *Click.*

"Sickmub the dog!" *Click.*

"To our adopted highway!" *Click.*

"To the old eagle," I said to Big L, who winked and clicked back with me.

Connie wasn't the only one who got adopted. Mr. Cator and his wife asked Josh if he wanted to come live with them. He got his own bedroom with a big empty box in it. Josh slept in the box once or twice, but then changed to the bed. By the next school year, no one even remembered him as Josh-in-the-Box. He was Josh Cator, the nerdy kid, but nerdy in a son-of-a-science-teacher kind of way. I would put him at number twelve on the popularity list.

As for the Mighty Termite.

Mrs. McCrary kept her word and didn't call the social worker and scream, "Get this troublemaker out of here now." Big L did make one crack. One night, we were at the dinner table and he looked up, startled like something had finally sunk in. "Two of them at my table. Both my kids. Tree-huggers. The dog too!"

"Both my kids?" I asked.

Mrs. McCrary rubbed my head. "Both of them. Go and figure that. Termite, pass the gravy please."

I decided to stick around the McCrarys' house for a little while longer. Not forever. I'd never promise that.

Just until I was sure that Big Momma was 200 percent safe. Maybe until Striker got ready to go off and live in the forest. By then, lots of new trees will have taken root. One would be big and strong enough to hold a termite-sized kid. Striker could live in Big Momma, and I'd set up in a nearby tree. We'd be neighbors.

Until then, I had plenty of experiments to keep a ball of energy like me busy.

Can a redwood tree grow from a cone if you talk to it every day?

Will Ike, a pill bug from the city, make friends with a dog from Forest Glen?

Can an outsider become an insider?

I guess I already have an answer for that last one.

WITHDRAWN